ECO FALLS

By: Ronald Wynn

ECO FALLS

ECO FALLS

By: Ronald Wynn

Ronald Wynn Productions, LLC

Ronald Wynn Productions, LLC

ISBN-10:0-9755284-3-2

ISBN 978-0-9755284-3-3

www. Penofpoet. com

Cover Design: Ronald Wynn

Editor: Miriam Rowan, Angie Hewitson

Manufactured in the United States of America

I walk this earth with an emptiness

That someday shall be restored.

I love and miss you Mom.

Maralyn Wynn

1936-2003

ECO FALLS

By: Ronald Wynn

TO THE TOP

Stefan reached past the woman in the blue business suit and pushed number 40 on the keypad. Like a Bingo chart, the numbers lit up in a diagonal pattern; there were at least 15 people in the elevator who already had made their choice. Stefan chuckled as he watched the numbers flash.

Stefan whispered, "Bingo"...anything, to try to keep his mind off the next few minutes.

Even though the height of the building was only 40 floors, Stefan was an architect, which meant he always knew exactly how high he was off the ground. In fact, he was the architect for this very building, and a well-known rising star in the world of designing buildings and skyscrapers. This was a special project for Stefan, as it was the first major project he had done solo out of college. He named his solo debut, "The Falls."

The reason he chose to name his project The Falls, was that every time the elevators went down, it looked like water falling from the top of the building. The entire face of the building was glass. The elevators were on the *exterior,* which was different from most towers in Boston. As the elevators descended, white lights in the shaft would turn on, chasing the elevator car to the ground. From a distance, you would constantly see the streaks of white light coming off of the top of the building and chasing the elevator. When the elevators returned upwards, the lights went dark, all you would see is the green color of the glass. The building was the talk of Boston. Other cities called on Stefan to build a similar building.

He was a guest on *20/20*, *Good Morning America,* and was the subject of a featured article in several national magazines. Because of this building and others, Stefan was chosen to create another building for downtown Boston. This new building would be the heart, body and soul of the city. The only problem for Stefan was the location of the meeting to discuss the plans...the penthouse of The Falls.

As an architect, Stefan was familiar with every piece of material used in constructing a building. He was familiar with all the possibilities of failure. He was afraid of heights more than the possibility of construction errors. He built a 40-story glass building, but he chose to live on the second floor in his condominium. That way, he could jump out if necessity dictated. Like an astronaut sitting on a fuel tank...waiting to be launched into space, Stefan was starting to feel the pre-launch jitters. The anxiety; knowing that one is sitting on enough fuel to fill more than 5,000 cars. Or worse—the fact that someone is igniting that fuel might cause a person to worry about every possibility of things going terribly wrong.

That's how Stefan felt each time he entered a building. He knew every danger that existed in construction, every variable that might happen in an unpredictable world: earthquakes, sediment shifts, storms...everything that could possibly compromise the design of the building. Stefan inventoried the dangers over and over...and over again. Therefore, taking the elevator to the 40th floor was not a simple task for him. His shirt absorbed his perspiration like a sponge; he felt that familiar taste invade his mouth...

That nasty flavor of..."I am fixing to pass out."

Some people call it dry mouth. It's irrelevant what you call it, the bottom line is, if you have ever passed out before, you recognize symptoms as an alert that your system is going to shut down.

Stefan loosened his tie and began to look around at the other passengers in the elevator. Some saw his fear and recognized his discomfort while others were so self-absorbed in their own personal drama that Stefan's worry managed to avoid their radar. Though he was in a room with 15 other people, close enough that the slightest movement guaranteed physical contact with a complete stranger, Stefan was alone. The elevator was a reflection of his life; although there were often many people around him, he was, indeed, alone.

Today he was going to the penthouse, to the top of the world if, of course, he could stay conscious for the elevator ride to the 40th floor. Stefan scanned the elevator in a desperate attempt to find something—anything to keep his mind off the ride to the top of the building.

He noticed a strikingly beautiful young woman who looked out of place. Instead of wearing the typical businesswoman's attire—a suit or a tight dress, she wore what looked like field clothes, and she wore them well.

Stefan's first thought was that she must be with OSHA. However, after second glance he concluded... *Nope, too pretty to be a pit bull.* Then, he saw the name on the side of her shirt...C.A.L.S... Stefan was familiar with the company. C.A.L.S. was an environmental company, funded primarily by government grants. The C.A.L.S. acronym stood for Clean Air, Land and Sea.

She was holding many folders in her arms awkwardly, reminding Stefan of a college student who was still perfecting her organization skills. She did not seem to be wearing makeup, and her hair was pulled back past her ears. Stefan glanced at her body. She had an hourglass figure that was sleek and slender and pleasing to look at.

Reality set back in as Stefan felt the sickness coming over his body again. Though he knew others had noticed his unease, Stefan caught her looking at him. Once he realized he had her attention, he turned into a mime. He looked out the window, and then put his hands over his eyes as if to block his sight from their looming ascension. When he put his hands down, she was laughing...and then she smiled.

Stefan's heart beat out of control. He forgot the elevator and forgot the street as he watched it shrink smaller and smaller as they climbed higher and higher. All he saw was her smile…blue eyes, brown hair, lips perfect for a television commercial. For the first time, a stranger caused his heart to beat erratically. Never before in his life had a woman caused him to forget his fear of heights.

In fact, not in high school, college or even as an adult was he ever able to ride in an elevator without struggling all the way up. Now, he felt faint, yet, it was not the height, it was the beautiful woman who just smiled at him. He leaned back against the wall of the elevator. The icy cold of the stainless steel felt like a defibrillator that provided sudden and much needed regulation for his body. He marveled silently… *She smiled at me...this incredibly beautiful woman smiled at me.*

He wanted to talk to her. His heart sank when the elevator stopped, as more people got off. The young architect was certain he was watching his window of opportunity slip away each time the elevator doors slid shut. Then Stefan smiled—she was still on.

The elevator climbed a few more floors, opening for another group to move on with their day and yet, the mesmerizing young lady did not move. Stefan breathed a sigh of relief, uttering, "Yes." She turned to him and smiled. He was on cloud nine. Not only did she smile but she just heard him acting like a high school kid, yet she smiled at him anyway.

There were only three other people left in the elevator with Stefan and the young woman. Three numbers still illuminated the elevator's panel: 23, 38 and 40. Stefan had previously met each of the board members that were attending the meeting so he didn't think anyone in the elevator was going to the 40th floor. He hoped they would all get off at 23 except her.

The elevator stopped and two walked across the threshold, heading to their destinations. The young woman caught onto the fact that he seemed happy when people left. She started to laugh, in fact, she turned her head to gain control of herself.

Stefan was on a roll. One more stop before they reached the 40th floor. If she stays, she must be going to the penthouse. The elevator stopped and the last person disappeared down the hallway, Stefan was so elated. His hope had come true... she was going the penthouse.

Then, without warning, the young woman waved at Stefan and stepped out into the corridor as well.

He was crushed. He felt like a child who just helplessly witnessed, in slow motion, his cherished triple scoop of chocolate ice cream fall off the cone, tumbling to the ground, and lost forever. He just stood there motionless, as the doors started to close.

Suddenly, he heard, "Oh crap! w-wait...wrong floor...wait please!"

Without thinking, he reached his hand into the closing door, stopping it just inches from closing. The young woman stepped back into the elevator. Stefan broke out in a huge smile… Imagine the smile of a young boy who was just handed a puppy, or was told, "Tomorrow we go to Disney Land." Stefan's smile was that big—from ear to ear.

"Guess you are going up?" Stefan inquired.

"Yes, I am... I'm Amanda Wilson."

Stefan heard the melodic sound of her voice but he was powerless to do anything other than watch her lips move.

Amanda paused a moment, waiting for Stefan to introduce himself, "And you are?" She asked.

It took a minute for Stefan to regroup, "Oh um me? I" (clearing his throat), he said, "I am Stefan Rogers."

Before he had time to say anything else, the elevator dinged and the door slid open. Amanda suddenly realized who he was; her heart beat out of control. She just rode 40 floors in the elevator with *Stefan Rogers*!

He designed this building, and was the chosen architect for the new project Boston had planned! Amanda was so excited she was certain her feet were no longer in contact with the floor.

She turned to say, "Hi," but the doors started to close.

Stefan nervously said, "We should head that way, nodding in the direction of the conference room.

Amanda smiled and started walking towards the doors of the conference room. Stefan followed her like a puppy. She could have zigzagged; he would have still followed her every move. He was clearly smitten by her voice, her looks, the way she smiled; everything else about her.

THE MEETING

Stefan followed Amanda into the meeting. There were ten 'suits,' a young woman who was an environmental engineer, and himself. Stefan was accustomed to the suits, because every project he created cost millions of dollars and somebody had to sign the check. That kind of money required financing from wealthy people. Often, Stefan felt out of place in these meetings.

A successful architect, Stefan had money, but the bottom line was that these people were influenced by power and wealth. Therefore, a young man with a little money, though he had more than anyone he knew his age, was not considered to have any knowledge in the world of finance. However, Stefan was not afraid of the money or power of others. Nor was he afraid to speak his mind or even just walk out.

Two years ago in New York, he was in a meeting where the suits turned on him, and they told him, "We are paying for this project and we will decide the general contractor!"

Stefan responded in a calm, matter of fact tone, "Then you won't build my building," and he walked out.

He vowed to never pick up the phone calls from a board that had shunned him. His Father taught him that a man's word is only as good as the grip of his hand. Stefan had been raised to respect others, and to do what he said he would do. He felt that if he held himself to such a high level of commitment and standard, that anyone he worked with should also have those same qualities.

Because of this, Stefan came across as very demanding and confident. He knew he had the ability to provide his clients with the very best their money could buy, but he was not willing to compromise his standards or principles.

That set Stefan aside from many other Architects, because he did not care about the fame. Even though he was sought after and known as one of the best, the suits would often come across very arrogant and stuffy; their personalities are not always accommodating to outsiders, those that are not part of society's elite.

Stefan sat and listened to each suit praise their credentials and status. One by one, they told of all the great projects they financed, and all the companies they bought and sold. Though he heard them, his attention was on the young woman in the peach colored North Face shirt who rode in the elevator with him. In fact, he could not keep his eyes off her. She wasn't arrogant self-involved, instead, she was quite or the opposite of most of the women he had met.

Stefan stood up and introduced himself as he normally did, a short speech, a list of his buildings and his commitment to excellence. He sat back down and noticed Amanda smile. He smiled back as the introductions continued around the room.

Then came the moment he was waiting for, Amanda stood and introduced herself.

"I am Amanda Wilson, an environmental engineer for C.A.L.S. We are contracted to make sure that the construction projects not only follow Government standards, but the solar foot print is held to the absolute minimum."

Amanda sat down. She turned toward Stefan. He was smiling. The woman in a suit next to him turned her head to look at Amanda. Stefan had been looking at her so long it drew attention. The lady was like a teacher catching a note passed between students, except this was just a smile, a simple smile

Though this was a two hundred Million dollar project, Stefan quickly lost interest in the meeting. He was more worried about how long it was going to continue. He looked down at his handmade watch, crafted from the metal of shackles that were worn by his Father in a P.O.W. camp in Vietnam. He wanted to be reminded of the cost of freedom every time he looked at the time. The hands moved the same as the first clock ever made...one second at a time.

Stefan uttered a sigh. Unfortunately, it was loud enough for Frank Goldsmith to hear. "Mr. Rogers, do you have something to add, are we keeping you from another appointment?"

Stefan replied, "No Sir, Mr. Goldsmith." "I um, apologize. I was disappointed in the stock market numbers, I just glanced at them. They are down."

What a save, Stefan thought to himself. He had brought up the one thing that was important to them. Money, and they forgot everything. Over the next few minutes, the suits talked about the market and what was the best strategy to save a slip, split reversal, you name it. They were covering all bases. Amanda looked at Stefan with an approving grin.

Silently, she mouthed, "Nice save!"

Stefan smiled. He never smiled in a meeting before, nor had he ever been so happy on the 40th floor, and in a glass room. They were served lunch. Like most costly meals, it was slightly bigger than an egg—a piece of chicken dressed with greens and rice. Stylish, but not filling.

The meeting lasted another hour, as the seconds ticked. Stefan knew the only way to talk to Amanda was away from the suits. After every meeting he was asked to stay awhile, because some of the investors wanted to talk about additions on their homes or about guest houses they wanted built on their islands.

Stefan wanted to get to know Amanda—the woman with a smile that touched his heart and soul. All he wanted to do is leave as soon as the meeting was over.

Stefan actually looked forward to the elevator ride down; something that he had never done before. This would be his chance to speak to her. The ice was broken upstairs in the meeting. Now they had something to talk about. As the meeting concluded, he kept his acceptance brief, explaining that it was a huge honor, and that he looked forward to adding to downtown.

The contract would only be granted if he was able to provide them with a detailed sketch showing how the new building would make driving through the city of Boston look like driving toward the mountains. Though this seemed like an impossible task, Stefan was the best in the country at creating master pieces. He was young, confident and delivered on his promises. He also charged accordingly. That might be why the suits chose him.

"In two weeks you will have your mountain, and I promise you will be moved," Stefan assured the suits as he stood up.

Stefan was not shy about his talent, He was a master in a field full of amateurs. Stefan was humble, but he knew what he could deliver, and he knew his clients would, and could, afford the best.

This project alone, would put over a million into his bank account, with a guarantee of two hundred thousand even if they pulled the plug and never constructed the building.

This was a great opportunity for the young architect. He knew he should have stayed after the meeting, but his mind was on Amanda. He shook hands, listening to the suits until he saw Amanda make her way into the lobby.

"I have to get to another meeting with OSHA... truly I apologize. I will see you in two weeks," he said, as he turned to catch up with the woman who moved his heart.

"Amanda, wait," Stefan called quietly as she was stepping into the elevator. Stefan did not notice the fact that she walked as slowly as she could, pretended to fix her shoe and stopped to take a picture of the view from the window, all in hopes of waiting for Stefan to ride down the elevator with her.

"Thank you for waiting."

"Wow! What a project, right? It looks like it will be a lot of fun," Stefan said.

Amanda looked at him smiling, and said, "Stefan I have to tell you, I have been in a lot of cities in my field of work. Honestly, I have never seen a building like The Falls before. I just don't have words to describe it. It is amazing. Clearly, you are a very deep man, and an incredible architect."

Stefan was lost in her words; not out of pride or flattery but her sincerity.

Amanda continued, "I haven't seen it at night, but this reminds me of Hickory Falls, four hours from here, near Eagle's Nest Mountain."

"Really? That sounds like a interesting place. Maybe I should take a look at that before I design the building for the project," Stefan suggested.

Amanda's heart was beating out of control.

"I would love to show it to you if you are interested," she told him.

Stefan smiled. "You know, that lunch wasn't much. Let's grab a bite to eat and talk about Eagle's Nest."

Amanda was not hungry, and even if she was, she was just too nervous to eat in front of him. She was not going to pass up a chance to spend time with Stefan Rogers. "I would love too," Amanda replied with a smile.

"Great! I know a place a couple blocks from here."

Suddenly, they stepped out of the elevator. Stefan stopped, slowly turned around and watched the doors of the elevator close. He was on the ground floor. He had ridden the elevator down from the 40th floor and never once realized it. He smiled, looked at Amanda and said, "That's a first."

"What?"

"Nothing…nothing," Stefan said with a smile.

WHO WAS AMANDA

Amanda grew up in a Southern Baptist family. She learned to give grace before she learned to stand. People called her "Mandy" for short, and she was very involved in the youth program at her church.

At a young age, the environment became a focal point in her life. From high school projects, to college reports, she was always bringing ecology to the forefront. The impact that man has on the planet, humanity's footprint, was important to her. Amanda became an environmental engineer, not because of the money. She felt it was a job which would empower her to keep an eye on big business and point out the impact that man had on the earth.

She was invited to intern for a prestigious environmental consulting firm, in Washington, DC. If you ask her about it, she will eventually tell you about the time that she ate lunch with the President of the United States. The luncheon took place in a private room away from the media and the public's eye.

She always felt that the president was not only misguided, but he clearly had shown no interest in the impact man was having on the environment. That evening, to her shock, the president was a voice for the environment. In a room full of people he spoke honestly about his concerns...gave his opinion and supported eco-friendly companies.

"To change the course that the world is traveling, laws would have to be passed not only by America, but the world," he said, as though he addressed a television. "I want change but I do not see the American people stepping forward to fight for that cause."

Amanda spoke up. "Sometimes, the world needs someone like you to start the conversation."

The room got quiet, people froze, waiting for a reply from the president. You could hear a pin drop.

"Young lady, I disagree with you. I think the world would listen to *you* before they would listen to me. I believe that people look at us in Washington as if we are only concerned with big business and winning elections, not as people who care about tomorrow."

Then the President looked Amanda in the eye and said, "Amanda, I believe in your passion. I see it in your eyes, but I don't see it in the eyes of the American people. They are self-absorbed and fail to lead. Instead, they follow. There are far too many who give advice, and far too few people like you, who actually do something about what they feel. To change the course of a train you need a track laid."

He went on to say that if he truly controlled Washington, the world would be a cleaner place. Like most young people mesmerized by fame and authority, Amanda's eyes filled with tears.

She was not so naive as to think that the President of United States would step forward and make policies that would change the way businesses ran in America, but here was a man of power speaking for the silent. To date, it has been the most memorable conversation about the environment she has ever had.

She thought of the strong men who wrote the Declaration of Independence, and men like Martin Luther King and Schindler. She wondered, what is the difference in a man who admits the wrongdoing of society and a man that causes change?

After college Amanda took a job with a firm near Boston that oversaw construction of all new buildings in large cities for the government. Their focus was the environmental impact of new construction, the danger to air-quality, and the surrounding vegetation.

However, Amanda's real passion was hiking and spending her time in the wild. Tree hugger, environmentalist. Call her what you will, but she truly believed in trying to save the planet. Many of the meetings where she spoke, required her to change the way people thought about the world around them.

She used PowerPoint presentations, physical samples and videos to show her clients—not only what they were doing wrong—but also to show them how to accomplish their jobs cleaner and more efficiently. Her good looks always caused a stir, however men quickly lost sight of her looks when she spoke. She was not a woman who used her sexuality to change minds. She possessed a strong understanding of the industry she represented, and she was able to convey this.

She frequently knew confidential corporate data about the companies' waste and pollution output that not even the CEO's knew. This often ended flirtation before it started. She was described as a bear, wolf or shark... for that reason men never challenged her knowledge and often told her they were impressed after the meeting. She was excellent at taking suggestions and applying them, resulting in major changes in the way companies operated.

Amanda felt God opened the door for her, and that she was put on this earth to be the spokesperson for the environment. Late December of last year, Boston decided they wanted the city to stand out even more since the construction of The Falls. In fact, it was because of The Falls, that Boston was going in a new direction. The city officials wanted their city to look as if it was nestled in the mountains from a distance.

"Come Back to Boston Where Heaven Awaits."

The purpose of the new slogan was to bring visitors to the city. They were looking for something that would stand out, not just from a car or street, but from the sky. Boston hoped that people would be drawn to the city because of the view, just like they visit Colorado and Wyoming. The city itself would no longer reflect a downtown of steel and stone but a city with a visual impact, presence, and a feeling of energy. The goal was for people to feel like they were standing next to a waterfall or the edge of a mountain.

Boston knew what they wanted, and they were willing to pay the price. Concerning to all, were the legal issues, and the impact on the environment. They called in C.A.L.S. (Clean Air, Land and Sea) to oversee the project. Their job was to let Boston know what the government would expect and what funding they could receive if they followed certain guidelines. Amanda was the spokesperson for C.A.L.S.; she had a proven track record. This was the company's largest job to date. They told her if they land the account they would make her the vice president, in charge of North America. This was a huge opportunity for her. Amanda was elated to receive the challenge.

How does one take the world of metal, steel and brick and make it feel and look like you're standing in the wilderness? Amanda remembered two years ago when the city built The Falls, she was concerned how it would eventually look. Would it change the city for the better or would it stand out as something strange and intrusive? She was amazed by its accomplishment; moved by the fact that a young man was able to create something that actually touched her as deeply as it did. This was a man who lived his entire life under the structure of numbers, weight and size.

She never thought she would respect the work of an architect as much as she respected the man who designed The Falls. This was now a building that was the symbol for greatness and freedom of thought. She was overwhelmed with joy at the opportunity to work on this project and to be associated with an architect she actually respected and thought was amazing.

FINALLY TIME ALONE

When they reached the restaurant, Stefan and Amanda were immediately seated by a window. Amanda could tell that Stefan had been there before, and the management clearly treated him as though he deserved their respect.

Stefan was desperate to know more about Amanda. Even though he was not a worldly man in the sense of dating a lot, he understood that if a woman said "yes," to dinner, she was interested in spending time with you.

Stefan was smiling. He couldn't help but smile. He was spending time with this woman who intrigued him.

The waiter came to their table, and after an awkward pause, they each ordered a glass of wine. Stefan could not take his eyes off of Amanda. She was so incredibly beautiful, inside and out.

As the waiter walked away Amanda spoke up, "Stefan, I have to tell you how incredible your buildings are. You must be so proud of your work. For me it is like looking at a work of art, colors blending in with the buildings…a reflection of the passing of another day. The way you use the blue lights during the day and the white lights at night, is just astounding. You truly out did yourself."

Stefan didn't say a word. He sat there and smiled. It's one thing to read article after article, even hear people on the media talk about how impressive your building is, but it is an entirely different thing to have a beautiful woman you're interested in, tell you how your work has moved her heart and soul. There was no ego involved. It was an affirmation that he was able to translate the images he saw in his head into a final product. Stefan often told his friends, the day he cannot create something that moves him, something that causes his heart to beat... will be the day he gives up being an architect.

Stefan was his own worst critic; he was overly critical and demanding, beyond any investor or committee. His name was on every project that he worked on. But more importantly, these buildings had to stand the test of time. They were an example, not only of his work, but who he was as a person and as an artist. His goal was for every building he created to be equal to or better than the one before. There was no room for failure. His standards and expectations exceeded even those of the people who paid for the projects.

Amanda's compliments made him smile, not only on the surface but even in his soul. Amanda could tell. She saw the look in his eyes and knew he was genuine.

Stefan told Amanda, "I've never spent much time in nature, but what I have seen moves me. I regret my career has kept me in the cities all the time. Tell me more about what you do. What causes do you believe in? What are your dreams?"

Amanda looked at Stefan. There was a long pause; perhaps she was caught off guard by his interest. Most of the men who took Amanda to dinner talked about themselves and their accomplishments. It was almost as if Amanda scared them, and made them feel like they were in competition; that in some way they had to prove that they were as successful, if not more.

Stefan asked her what makes *her* happy and how she ended up working in the industry of her choice. Amanda had to look away. There was something in Stefan's eyes that caused her body to tingle. An attraction she had not felt in a long time. She was afraid if she looked at him, he would see how he was affecting her. He genuinely cared. The fact that he wanted to know more about her caused her heart to race.

Ah, saved. The waiter returned to the table,

"Are you ready to order?"

"I think I'll have the salmon salad," Amanda said with a smile.

"I'll have the same," Stefan told the waiter.

They closed the menus and handed them to the waiter. The energy between them was so strong that even the waiter smiled before he walked away

Stefan was excited to hear more about Eagle's Nest.

"Amanda do you think you could get away this weekend and drive up to Eagle's Nest? I am interested in seeing it."

Amanda had a very busy schedule, but the fact that she would get to spend more time with Stefan caused her to react instead of think. "I would love to go up there. In fact, I have a friend who owns a cabin about a half hour away where we could stay, if you want to see some of the others sites like Hickory Falls?"

Stefan could not help but grin. It was like he was a teenager again, which in turn, caused Amanda to grin. "I think that it sounds like an awesome adventure," he told her.

"Great! I will call Samantha and see if we can stay there this weekend... I am sure she won't mind. She will likely ask a lot of questions about you, but she is cool," Amanda said. Thinking of the answers to Samantha's questions caused her to start to smile uncontrollably.

It was a great evening. A time to get to know a person who made your heart beat out of control. It was so obvious—the attraction between the two—that people would look at them and smile. Stefan and Amanda noticed the attention. They had that look, the look that the main characters always have in a romantic movie. Where everyone is sitting there, screaming at the television, "Go ahead and kiss her! Can't you see she wants you to kiss her?" It was an energy that neither had felt in a long time, they both were very nervous. As the night flew by it was obvious there was a deep attraction between them.

After dinner, they sat there and watched the sun set among the buildings. Amanda was amazed how the orange colors reacted with the different building material. How the light bounced and illuminated the surrounding windows and doors.

Stefan smiled as he watched the setting sun in her eyes. He felt this was the start of something incredible.

Though they had not touched or kissed it felt as though this was something they did together often. A dinner out, a sunset and a glass of wine...what more could two people want out of life?

It had been a long day, and Amanda had much to do before the weekend. She looked at her watch. "Stefan, I have had such a great time, but unfortunately I have a meeting at seven in the morning. Do you mind if we call it a night?"

Stefan was disappointed, that time had gone by so quickly.

"Amanda I had a great time too. I look forward to working with you on this project." They walked back toward The Falls, laughing and talking, then Amanda stood still, frozen, looking up at the building.

"Stefan that is incredible! It's so much more than I would have imagined! How in the world did you come up with that design?"

Amanda was looking at The Falls in action. She was watching the elevators go down, and the lights coming on like water cascading over the top of the building. She was absolutely mesmerized, not only by the sheer beauty—but also the fact that Stefan drew this from a dream. They were standing close together, and somehow they ended up holding hands. Just hours earlier they were strangers, but it seemed their souls desperately wanted to unite. As Amanda watched the elevators, she shook her head.

"Pretty cool isn't it? Sometimes I go out on my balcony and I just sit and watch the elevators go down. Believe it or not, I get the same feelings that strangers do when I watch it," Stefan said.

"Well it's simply amazing Stefan, simply amazing."

They reached the parking garage and the valet went to get Amanda's car. In that moment they started to feel awkward... They both wanted to kiss, yet they were strangers, united by a heartbeat. Stefan squeezed Amanda's hand tightly.

"You are an amazing woman, and I can't wait for this weekend. I want to know everything about you," Stefan told her.

Amanda smiled. She desperately wanted to jump into his arms and hold him but she knew that it was too soon. She told him goodbye and climbed into her car. As she drove off she could not help but look into the mirror at the man with whom she had become instantly infatuated with.

STEFAN'S PAST RELATIONSHIPS

Stefan did not feel complete even though he had the world at his feet. A young and attractive man, he looked the part, dressed well, received invitations to all the important functions—but inside he was lost. He spent his whole life perfecting his talent. He never made time for feelings.

Women certainly chased after him, but he never took the time to get to know them. He would always find an excuse not to be in town. Stefan always ended the relationship before it reached the 'moving in' stage. He was not a virgin, but he had only been with four women in his life. The first, when he was in high school, one in college and the other two, trying to find happiness.

Though Stefan believed in commitment, he was the first person to tell you to run. He felt that he was a bad bet; the future only meant that you were going to get hurt. Stefan was attracted to women, but he kept his mind on his job and avoided anything that would lead to a relationship.

His friends lived to party, but Stefan was not interested. He still had values. He believed that one day he would find a woman that only belonged to him; her body only touched by his. It seemed that in his world, loyalty and respect were hard to find, that passion meant sex. Stefan did not believe that.

When you are a well-known, up and coming architect, you attract the best looking women; the ones who are groomed from a young age to seek out wealth and power. There are women who spend thousands of dollars tucking and tightening everything so a man with money might find them desirable.

Stefan came from a family that stayed together for love, not money or looks. Though his father at one time, was an attractive young man, being in a P.O.W. camp in Vietnam took all the boyish charm away. The starvation he endured, deprived him of his muscle mass and smile, but Stefan's mother loved him as though he had never changed. An illness called war, and a hell called Vietnam, was a nightmare that has lived in their family Stefan's entire life.

Stefan learned the value of love and relationship from his parents. He also understood the impact of life and friends... how they can cause problems in a relationship. He knew that he did not have time to work on a relationship and the projects that he had planned, so he gave up on finding love. In fact, he simply turned the other direction every time he thought it got close. Co-workers and friends filled his pockets with phone numbers to call, but for Stefan, they were just ink on a page, names that belonged to strangers.

Though he was doing what he felt best, Stefan was alone—no one knew how truly lonely he was inside. He had a warm, friendly smile; one that caused you to want to have a conversation with him. But beyond that there was a sadness not seen by most. He had a longing to belong to something.

Money was not the driving force for Stefan to become an architect. As a child he loved to build things. His family was barely middle class; they were not well connected in society. Everything that Stefan had accomplished came from hard work. Stefan going to one of the best architectural colleges in the nation was only possible because of the huge sacrifices that his mother and father made.

Stefan was taught early on that everything had a price; he realized that nothing in life was free. He understood that even in relationships there was a price or commitment that had to be there for it to work. How could you be with someone? How could you love someone so deeply if you were not willing to work things out? All the relationships that he had were on the surface. The women were attracted to his fame, his wallet, or his looks. People constantly told him that he was with the wrong type of a woman. You're going to the wrong types of places, they would say.

Stefan never intentionally went anywhere to meet a woman. He would be out with his friends, and all of a sudden a girl started talking to him and started filling that void in his heart that was missing—attention. It did not take much for him to get distracted, though often, it led only to him getting hurt. His emotions kicked in. The longing to be touched took the place of logic and reason. It usually lasted about a month before he saw the true colors.

The phone calls would eventually get less frequent, and the personal time turned into social gatherings. They all ended the same. Stefan found reasons to spend less and less time with them. They never seemed to last, Stefan wasn't interested in sex.

He had not based his opinion on biblical principle, but more on the simple fact that there are many diseases and issues that arise from being intimate with a person. Stefan was only willing to share his body with a woman he felt was going to be *the one*. The option for spontaneous sex was not found in a logical thinking person's brain. Stefan was all about logic.

The women that Stefan was meeting, were not who he needed in his life. Stefan was a target. Not only was he attractive and well dressed, but most of his friends knew of his wealth and tried to take advantage of it. It's impossible to say the last time one of Stefan's friends bought dinner or the tickets to a game. Not that it mattered to Stefan, because he was not stingy with his money; it's just the simple fact that Stefan was the meal ticket for a lot of his friends.

He was not interested in going through life just to party. Deep, down inside, Stefan wanted to be in love and to share eternity with his soul mate.

AMANDA VS STEFAN

Their relationship started not as a fairytale, but a tragedy. A need for two people to find happiness, lost in a world that consumed their souls. Two hearts, lonely and desperate with the need to feel alive, searched to find happiness in a world that had taken it away.

Amanda had a strong up-bringing, she believed in love, but after years of men constantly pursuing her, she got tired of the constant advances. The men she encountered were the product of the new America, the new way of treating a woman. Amanda found most men to be socially degrading and condescending toward women.

Like Stefan, Amanda too, was worn down. People wonder, how two worlds so different can come together and find happiness? Finding fulfillment means one must first admit longing for someone, realizing the present need.

Stefan and Amanda had both reached a point in their lives where they were looking to fill that need…maybe not on the surface, maybe it was more of a thought, yet subtly exposed.

No, they both knew better. They both had successful careers but were alone inside. Very few people have the ability to go through life alone and remain happy. Many people who express they are happy alone are just covering up the pain. Yet, deep inside they wish for a partner…someone that loves them and believes in them. Even those people long to find the one thing that completes them, a soul that understands them and loves them in return.

Amanda fell in love with her high school sweetheart Bobby. She continued to date him while she was in college. Bobby and she became intimate right before he left for boot camp. He'd convinced her that if she truly loved him she would give herself to him so those memories would get him through their time apart. Bobby was killed in a car wreck heading home for leave the following Christmas. Amanda built a wall so high that no man was able to get close until now.

Stefan was incomplete. He had the entire world at his feet, yet he felt empty inside. Though he was known as one of the brightest young architects, it did not change the magnitude of loneliness that he felt. Stefan flashed an incredible smile; he was handsome and full of personality and charm. But, if you had the ability to read the soul, if you could look into his eyes, you would see his loneliness. Some people called it sadness, but the truth is that it is the shadow cast by a soul that is missing love.

COUNTING THE MINUTES

It was Tuesday night, and there were only a couple days before the trip. Stefan picked up the phone and called Mike, one of his buddies, who was an avid outdoors man. "Where can I find some *real* hiking clothes?" he asked. Mike joked with him..."Who are you buying them for, because I know you are afraid of heights and wild animals?"

Stefan knew the sarcasm was coming. He did not go into great detail and just told Mike it was for one of his projects and he needed to have the right clothing. Mike gave him the name of a sporting goods store on the south side of Boston, who had a good reputation for carrying a large selection of quality gear.

Stefan could not stop thinking about Amanda. He got up early Wednesday morning and made plans to go shopping. An architect is similar to a writer, once you get to a certain status in your career, no one asks you what time you are coming to the office, because they realize most of your work is done at home. More than one night a week, you will work until the sun rises again. Stefan's mind was not on the new project. It was on Amanda. He wanted to make sure that he was not only dressed properly but he looked good in the outfits he picked out.

Stefan knew everything about fashion. He felt God gave him the money, so the responsible thing to do would be to buy quality. By the time he got home Wednesday night, he owned several new outfits, including the latest gear to carry his water and supplies. Though he trusted Amanda, he also bought a top-of-the-line GPS—just in case.

Stefan wanted to talk to Amanda on the phone, but he was afraid she would think that he was being too aggressive, so he decided to text her. He told her he was looking forward to the trip, and that he felt this would be an opportunity for him to learn more about nature and have a broader concept of what the city of Boston was looking for. He pushed send, and as it disappeared off the screen, he desperately wanted to take it back. He was worried that it sounded too serious; too much about business.

"Why didn't I say how beautiful she was or what a great time I had together with her?" he shook his head, Stefan was an emotional mess. No other woman ever caused these feelings in Stefan.

The phone rings...

Stefan just finished sending the message. In fact, he was still contemplating whether he did the right thing or not. His phone rang again. He raced across the room, because he believed it might be Amanda. He grabbed the phone, picked it up and looked at the screen. He was disappointed, but only for a moment. It was his mother calling. Her voice always calmed him down when the storms came in his life. Every time he heard her voice he felt like he was home again.

"How's my baby doing?"

"Hi Mom, how's Dad?"

"He is fine...he misses you."

She started telling him the stories that seem to be recordings played over and over, every time she called. She told him about the same aunts and uncles getting into fights or disagreements over and over again. She would always tell him, "The house seems empty without you," and ask " When are we going to see you again.? You know, it's been a long time." "I miss you," she continued, sounding sad.

"I know Mom, it has been really busy...I might stop by late Sunday, but I can only stay for a couple hours. I'll be up in your direction."

His mother's voice changed—you could hear the excitement. "Stefan, you can stay as long as you want, you could spend the night if you'd like."

"No Mom, I need to get back to town. I will have a friend with me." His mother knew, the fact that he did not say a guy's name meant he would have a female companion.

"Is there something you want to tell me about this girl, Stefan?" His mother always knew how to get information out of him.

"I think she might be the one, mom. I'm just trying to tell you that she's special mom, she makes my heart beat out-of-control." Stefan didn't mind his mom knowing that he had affection for this girl, but his father was a different story.

"Bob... Bob, Stefan found the girl of his dreams."

"Mom… don't tell Dad! I just met her, and you know how he will want to question everything, try and find out every little detail about her."

His father was the one who would always ask awkward questions, demanding answers about 'How long the relationship has been going on? What does this lady see in you?' Stefan was successful and his father knew that. It seemed all the pressure and questions were because he was concerned about people taking advantage of his son. He figured if he asked them tough questions in front of Stefan…if they really liked him, they would answer. If not, he would get a sense of who they really were. But this cross examination was awkward and sometimes embarrassing for Stefan. Unless he truly felt he was interested in a woman he would not bring her around his family anymore.

So, in the course of the last 10 years, only one girl since high school ever came to the house. And in her case, the demise of the relationship was more about Stefan not being ready to settle down than it was about her character or anything she did wrong.

Stefan's mother was excited—it was as if he was coming home for Thanksgiving. Before Stefan could even finish talking, his mother started describing the meal she was planning to make. Stefan knew any opportunity to see his mom was special, but he wanted to end the conversation to see if Amanda responded to his text.

"Mom, I'm expecting a phone call, but I want you to know that I love you very much. I'll give you a call Sunday, when we are on the way to let you know what time to expect us. Tell Dad I love him and I look forward to seeing you both on Sunday."

"Wait Stefan... What is her name?"

"Amanda, Mom. Her name is Amanda."

"Oh my, that's a beautiful name Stefan. You tell her that we look forward to seeing her and that our home is her home."

"Okay, Mom. I have to get going. I love you."

Stefan hung up the phone, with a smile on his face for two reasons, one: he was thinking about Amanda, and two: his mom was going to meet this incredible woman that he can't seem to get out of his mind.

AMANDA ON HIS MIND

Though it was Wednesday night, and he was ready to go for Friday, he felt Friday was too far away. He did not feel obsessive, but he desperately wanted to see her again.

He called her cell phone and left a message...

"Amanda, this is Stefan. I was wondering if we could possibly get together sometime tomorrow. I have some ideas about the project I would like to discuss with you. We can have coffee, breakfast or lunch. Whatever works for you."

As he hung up the phone, he felt like a kid in high school. He couldn't help but smile when he thought of the possibility of seeing her again.

Amanda had been in a meeting with her phone on *vibrate*. When she looked down and saw that Stefan was calling, her face lit up with a smile, even though she couldn't answer. She couldn't wait for the meeting to be over to run out into the hallway like a high school girl. She saw the text earlier but was unable to read it, so when she saw she also had a voice mail from Stefan she was elated.

An hour later, when the meeting finally broke, she was able to check the message. Like a teenager in love, she was oblivious to everything and everyone around her. She was ecstatic, Amanda quickly replied and told Stefan that an early lunch tomorrow would work out great; she too, had some ideas to share.

She pushed send and felt her heart beat as though they were talking on the phone. Just like Stefan, she was in love. It would be nice to say that Stefan was busy working on a project or getting stuff ready for his trip, but the truth is, the phone was on his mind.

More importantly, when was he going to see her again? He couldn't wait for an answer. When the text chimed, he raced across the room to check his phone. Just by the smile on his face one could easily guess it was Amanda. He was grinning from ear to ear, not only was she meeting him for lunch, but she also clearly wanted to see him.

He returned the text and told her to meet him at the coffee shop on Hanover Street at 11:00 AM. The shop had coffee and great food, it was a good choice to give Amanda a taste of Boston's culture. He continued with the message and told her he would be the man with a smile on his face. He felt butterflies in his stomach when he sent the text.

Amanda was no longer in the meeting and still had the phone in her hand. Maybe she didn't have time to put it back down, or maybe she was just as bad as Stefan, and couldn't wait for his reply. When her phone chimed, her smile was bigger than life. She read his acceptance out loud as if telling the world she was so lucky. When she read the part about the man with the smile, her heart beat faster and she stomped her feet in jubilation. She knew at that moment that Stefan was truly interested in her.

When you are madly in love with someone and they respond in a way that tells you that they too, are interested in you, it is the greatest feeling in the world. You know by their response that there is no place in the world they would rather be than by your side, across the table or walking hand-in-hand in the park. Amanda knew Stefan wanted to spend time with her as badly as she wanted to spend time with him.

The next morning, she woke up and dressed. But, this morning she took a little longer fixing her hair, making it perfect. She looked at her eyebrows and checked her teeth. This morning there was a different feeling in the air, she had butterflies in her stomach for the first time in years.

Like her first date in high school, she was worried about what she was going to wear. She tried on several outfits, trying to pick out what she felt he would like. She knew he was into fashion; he dressed well, so she was worried if she dressed too casually it might turn him off.

Though she had nice outfits, she never found a reason to follow the latest trends. She usually dressed for a lecture or a hike. It was rare that she was going to dinner with a man because of a date. Even though the meeting was supposed to be about the upcoming project, she felt the same way Stefan felt—this was a date.

Stefan woke up earlier than usual. As the coffee pot gurgled, and the sun climbed above the edge of the city, Stefan danced around his condo to music. This was not normal behavior for Stefan.

His life was about consistent, redundant behavior... As an artist, many times he was bored at corporate functions, lectures about how much money was to be spent and how fast the job was to get done. Stefan was the architect, the commander-in-chief of the project.

So, even though he didn't want to be part of the business meetings, he was forced to attend most, if not all of them. He remembered one time last year, he sent his secretary instead.

The CEO was so irritated that he called him on his personal cell phone and told him, "If I have to sit through these damn meetings, so do you, Mr. Rogers! If you miss one more meeting I will pull your contract."

Stefan learned that even though his talent was sought after, he still had to follow the rules of the game. Today, there was no board meeting, no lecture or budget meeting. There was no one to answer to. Today was all about getting to know Amanda. This was simply a lunch with a beautiful woman to talk about a future that, he hoped included her.

Stefan was not known for being on time. Like many artists, he always had a thousand things going on. Being on time was always a challenge for Stefan. He was always in a hurry and always running behind. This morning he was not only up an hour early, but he was dressed and walking around singing, clearly the sign of a man in love.

The morning flew by. It was time for them to meet downtown. Even though coffee shop was busy, Stefan had no problem finding Amanda's smile. There was this energy between them just standing next to each other; it looked like they had been married for years. It was not a sad "I'm stuck with this guy look," but a look of devotion, caring and attentiveness that is only found in the heart of true love.

When they got to the table, neither one could stop smiling. Like a child sitting in front of the Christmas tree waiting to open presents, they both beamed with radiant smiles. Stefan reached across the table. Before his hand made it halfway, Amanda's hand met his. No words were said

They sat there for a long period of time just holding hands. Maybe it was a gesture, a greeting that was more than just hello. After a minute or two of holding hands and smiling, they questioned why their bodies wanted to touch even though they had not known each other very long.

Amanda slowly pulled her fingers out of Stefan's grip. It didn't change their feelings; it just set the rules of behavior. They both had been through so much; it seemed that they were destined to become lovers.

Amanda started talking first, "so you have some ideas that you would like to share with me? Stefan, I've spent the last 15 years of my life hiking the Appalachian Trail, walking in the wilderness and watching the sun set in the mountains. I'm very familiar with the ambiance and energy of nature. I would love to hear your ideas about the project in Boston."

Stefan heard her talking but was, quite frankly, lost in her beauty. His heart was beating so loudly that her soft voice was hard to hear. He truly was in love with her. A woman he barely knew had walked into his life and change the way he breathed.

"Amanda, my goal is to add to the feeling of The Falls. I want people to come to Boston just as they go to the Appalachian Trail. I have not been there, but I've heard it is beautiful."

Amanda smiled because Stefan was talking about her backdoor, the very thing she loved more than life.

"I have spent most of my life hiking Eagle's Nest and Hickory Falls. That is an amazing part of the country. I can't wait for you to experience the sights and sounds that make up the wilderness...the beauty of God's creation," Amanda said as she looked deep into his eyes.

Stefan was excited to tell Amanda about the vision he saw in his dream the night before. Most of Stefan's ideas came from dreams. It wasn't that he was an oracle or a fortune teller, but he thought so deeply during the day, the only time his mind could actually respond was when everything shut down. During that time, his brain could expand on ideas and thoughts. In fact, Stefan kept a drawing pad by his bed. Two years ago he had a dream... one of the best he has ever had. He dreamed about an elaborate building over a small river. The structure was complex. He had solved several issues that have plagued him for years. It was an amazing work of art. The next day, when he awoke, he forgot the critical components. He could draw the basic idea but, he was still plagued with the issues that had always kept him from building a master piece like that over a river.

His dreams are almost like looking into the future, a world that has already solved all the questions before they ever got asked. "Amanda, I want you to close your eyes…"

Amanda closed her eyes and her body tensed. It wasn't the response Stefan wanted, he was just trying to help her visualize what he was going to say.

The truth was that she had fallen in love with Stefan. Closing her eyes so close to him caused the passion in her soul to speak up. "Amanda… think about The Falls… imagine from the right side of The Falls to the left there is a glass building that stretches in height past The Falls… not perfectly square or rectangle, but staggered. Imagine the building is made of orange glass. Different shades of orange. Not just solid orange, but a gradual shift in color, similar to the side of a mountain. It looks like the face of rock with textured, molded glass. You see the reflection of the elevators from The Falls against the orange. The new building has its own set of waterfalls, similar to a small stream that runs down the cracks of the mountain. These waterfalls are inside the building, not protruding outward, but inside the glass."

Amanda smiled...

Stefan continued to describe the things that he saw in his dream. Amanda could no longer keep her eyes closed. The sound of passion in his voice made her heart beat out of control. She looked at Stefan while he was sharing his story. She reached across the table, grabbed his hand, and held it tight.

A lunch that was only supposed to be an hour, turned into two. It was filled with laughter; more laid back than a dinner or coffee. This was truly a date. The time needed for Stefan to get to know Amanda. Two people together, talking about dreams and desires, and all the while, sizing each other up for character, likes and dislikes.

Amanda had been hurt badly in her past...something that Stefan had no idea about. Amanda questioned Stefan about relationships, the value of spending time together, and family. Stefan was inexperienced in the world of relationships. His questions were more focused on what Amanda expected in a man, spending time together, emotions and future plans.

They shared similar interests. Both earned a level of respect in their industries. They were brought together by chance, some might say, yet—neither believed that.

Amanda grew up a strong Christian. Her faith kept her path straight. Stefan was logical to a fault, believing that nothing happened by chance. They were two people who complimented each other. Yet, they both felt there was a divine influence. They came together out of the complexity of the world...an architect who built a world from man-made products and an environmentalist who wanted to protect the world from builders who did not care about their impact on the earth.

Stefan was different, not only did Amanda see this in the buildings he designed, but also his uncompromising choices for materials and the general contractors for the projects. He was not a silent voice. He was demanding and firm. Stefan's Father was a P.O.W. during the Vietnam War, so he grew up in a home that appreciated freedom and the ability to say what is on your mind and demand that people do as they are expected.

Stefan only allowed quality people to work on his projects. He never allowed corners to be cut or any disrespect to others from his workers. It did not matter if one was putting mud on blocks, or a designer in a three piece suit; Stefan demanded respect for everyone.

Amanda felt comfortable around Stefan because many men his age were still boys; they had no direction and stood for nothing. Amanda and Stefan moved forward faster than either one thought would ever happen.

At the table waiting for their meal, Stefan held Amanda's hand, though she sat across from him. It was subtle, romantic, Stefan softly wrapped his hand around hers and continued to talk to her. Amanda's heart was beating so hard. No man had held her hand at a table since the days of saying grace as a child. She was afraid to pull it away. But even though she was nervous, she did not want him to let go.

Thoughts of Stefan holding her filled her mind. She reached up and ran her hand through her hair, more for something to distract the physical thoughts in her mind than the need to adjust misplaced hair. Stefan loved the softness of her hand. He remembered shaking goodbye after the meeting. There were long pauses with them just staring at each other...their hearts were smiling.

A man walked up and asked, "How long have you two been married?" Amanda couldn't respond...

Stefan placed his finger up to his lips and said, "I have been keeping that a secret...someday soon I hope."

Amanda smiled. She couldn't help but smile. Grinning from ear to ear she *felt* his words. No other man impacted her in that way...touched her heart in that way. Though she just met Stefan a few days earlier, it was as if they had been together for years. She felt so comfortable around him, like he was a part of her.

Like holding a baby, she had a longing to just be with him, to hear his voice and lie in his arms.

Two o'clock came too soon. It was time for them to head back to work. As they walked outside holding hands, Stefan told Amanda how beautiful she looked. They both were as nervous as high school kids behind a forbidden building. Their bodies wanted more, but even though they were strangers, a newly found energy was forming.

Amanda offered…"My Car is around the side here. Do you want to walk me to it?"

Amanda was not waiting for an answer, because it was not really a question, but an invitation to spend every moment with Stefan she could. "I go where you go, young lady." Stefan swaggered—if that is the term—the proud walk of a man who knows his company is desired by a woman.

When they reached her car, Stefan told her he was looking forward to the trip. They confirmed the meeting place and time. Stefan had trouble standing still. As Amanda moved the keys around in her hand as though she could not find the one with the BMW logo, Stefan leaned forward, and like oxygen igniting fire, their lips found each other. Amanda sunk against the car door. Her body temperature rose. They unleashed something which lingered on the surface for the past hour and now it was free. Amanda could not help but moan which sounded like begging in Stefan's ear. Never before had he kissed a woman so softly and so deeply. Never had he so desperately wanted to taste the lips.

Amanda took a deep breath and placed her hands on his chest... "Wow! I um, I need to get back to the office Stefan..."

Stefan was breathing hard. She could feel the rapid beat of his heart beneath her hands. She wanted to rip off his shirt—to be taken in the back seat of her car. But instead, she leaned forward and kissed him again, this time she wrapped her arms around him and held his head in her hand.

They heard a cat-call whistle, and another. The construction workers across the street lost interest in repairing the sidewalk and found pleasure in cheering for the young couple. Both Stefan and Amanda started to laugh.

Stefan squeezed Amanda's hand..."Another Time."

"I will be counting the minutes," Amanda said.

Stefan smiled and waved good bye as Amanda watched his tight jeans rhythmically disappear around the corner. She sat in her car for a few minutes. Inside she was a wreck. Her body as hot as it had ever been. Yet, it was only a kiss. She looked in the mirror and fixed her lip-stick.

Stefan headed to his car, literally spinning in circles like he was on stage, tap dancing. They found each other in a crazy world full of fake people...two hearts that beat as one. Stefan thought about the kiss, and he could not stop smiling.

Of course, that night neither one slept much. They both kept thinking about the kiss. Stefan thought about how warm her breasts were against his chest, the softness of her lips and the moans that caused his heart to race. Amanda had never been held so softly, with so much passion. She felt the muscles beneath his shirt, the beating of his heart against her breasts. Clearly, they both felt tomorrow was going to be an exciting day, a day they both would never forget.

AMANDA CALLS HOME

Amanda was so in love with Stefan. There was nothing about the man not to love. He was intelligent, sweet, kind and most importantly, he cared about what she had to say, and what her plans for the future were.

Amanda was so excited about the trip she nearly forgot to call Samantha about staying in the cabin. Amanda walked back and forth on the balcony as she dialed. She had a perfect view of The Falls. She smiled each time the white lights chased the elevators down.

"Samantha, hey how are you doing? It's Amanda!"

"Hi, how is the trip, did you get to meet Stefan Rogers yet?" Samantha asked in an excited voice.

"You will not believe it. Sit down. No really. Sit down. I had dinner with him last night! He is so incredible. I have never met anyone like him."

"You're in love with him!" Samantha blurted out, interrupting Amanda's continual praise of Stefan.

"He is just so perfect, Samantha. I can't stop smiling around him."

"Take it slow," Samantha told her, not because she was worried, but because it was the traditional thing to say since they had just met.

"Samantha, I have a huge favor to ask. Can we stay at the cabin this weekend? He wants to go with me to Eagle's Nest."

Samantha started to laugh. "Girl you *are* in love with him! You have never spent the night there with a man before. You don't have to ask. The key is under the rock by the oak tree. Help yourself."

"You are the best Samantha. You're right. I think he is the one. Hey, I need to call Mom before she goes to bed. I will call you Sunday when we get back. Thank You!"

"You better take a lot of pictures, and I want to hear the whole story, when you get back. I want to know everything!" Samantha said almost like she was Amanda's sister. They were best friends in high school, even though it had been many years, they remained very close. Just like sisters.

Amanda never went on a trip without telling her Mom and Dad. One thing you learn as a hiker is that you have to make a travel plan so if something goes wrong, family or friends can search for you in the area you were hiking.

Amanda had been a part of many mountain rescues that turned into body recover missions, because for days they searched the wrong area due to the fact the hikers never filled out a travel plan beforehand. She had held parents and loved ones after the bodies had been found. It was something that she never wanted her parents to have to deal with.

There was always a danger of something going wrong, a loose rock causing a broken ankle or a broken bone, every medical issue that high up could turn deadly... even a simple accident, that far from a hospital could be life threatening. Amanda had been climbing for years, so safety was the most important thing. She dialed her mother, still smiling from the conversation with Samantha.

"Momma... Hey it's Amanda!"

"Hi, Sweetheart! How are you doing? How did the meeting at The Falls go?" her Mom asked.

"Momma it was awesome!"

"Well did you get to meet him?"

"Momma"... Amanda paused as though she was shy.

"Yes, I met him, and Momma... he is so incredibly awesome. We are going to Eagle's Nest this weekend. He wants to go see the mountains so he can get an idea of what the new building will look like."

"Amanda you sound happy, I haven't heard you this happy since...Bobby."

"I know Momma, it's crazy. I just met him a couple days ago but my heart has not stopped beating fast. He is everything that you told me Mr. Right would be. I am excited, I am scared... I am dizzy!"

"Take it slow baby. You sound happy, but take it slow."

"I know Momma, I am. I wanted you to know that we will be climbing Hickory Falls Friday and Eagle's Nest Saturday. I'll call you Saturday night by 10 pm"

"Ok Dear, I look forward to meeting this young man. You be careful, and make sure you watch the weather channel because we have had some bad storms rolling in lately."

"Yes Momma I always do, you know that. I will call you when we get in Saturday night. I Love you."

Amanda hung up the phone, leaned back against the wall and started thinking about Stefan. Though it had been years since a man had touched her heart in the shadows of a candle she found herself dreaming of him. After spending a wonderful evening together she could hear his voice in her head.

She closed her eyes and crossed her arms, feeling the warm skin. She imagined his hands holding her against the wall, unbuttoning her shirt, whispering in her ear. Her heart pounded, for a moment as she got lost in the fantasy of him making love to her...

She took a deep breath, more of a deep sigh, and she slowly walked down the hall to her room. She sat on the bed and laid back against the pillows. She could not get him off her mind, never before had she had these kinds of thoughts for a man that really was a stranger. It was as if they had known each other all her life.

She closed her eyes, and found herself held in his arms, nothing between them but the temperature of their skin. She was smiling as he whispered her name. It had been a long day and dream or not—she was in the arms of an incredible man.

In the morning she did not even remember going to bed, but she did remember how his arms felt around her in the dream. In only two hours she was going on the trip of a lifetime... Everything had already been packed and was in the car. She went out onto the balcony and watched the sun rise from beneath the city. It was finally time to head to The Falls.

THE TRIP

Stefan met Amanda in the lobby of The Falls. She was staying in town for the meetings and that was a location with which she was familiar. The only requirement Amanda had, was that Stefan would let go and give her his undivided attention for two days. Well, not so much give his attention to her, but to the world Amanda wanted him to see. Amanda was excited that he accepted her offer, and they were on their way.

She told Stefan upfront, because of her values, that they would be sleeping in separate rooms. She had Stefan for only two days, "Give me two days and I will show you a part of life that you have never seen before." She told him.

After their lunch date, she felt really good about Stefan. The further they drove away from the city, the further away from a forest of cold and lifeless cement... Amanda was left with just Stefan. The noises of the city were gone. The hustle and bustle were behind them, if only for a couple of days.

Now, it was quiet time with a man who moved her heart and soul...a man who caused her body to heat up with the mere sound of his voice. She thought of the initial energy she felt when they first met, how she was so happy. It seemed that her heart was right about Stefan.

To be clear, for Amanda, the attraction was not his worldly success, but his drive for excellence, his passion to touch people with his work, the fact that a building to him was a work of art, no less than paint to a painter...he was an artist.

Amanda watched the steering wheel slide through Stefan's hands. His forearms were clearly muscular. She thought of the kiss by the car, the look in his eyes. She tapped her lips with a closed fist and screamed, "Oh my gosh," inside her head. She knew this weekend was not going to be a simple hike.

Stefan broke the silence.

"Hey do you mind? I thought we could pull over and take a picture of the road ahead, a road with no buildings; kind of like an exodus from the city; the beginning of our life—I mean our journey—together."

Amanda did not miss a word, and though it seemed out of place he was talking about his future with her. Inwardly, she was screaming whoop, whoop—yes.

But outwardly she had to keep calm. "Sure, whatever you want to do, Babe."

Amanda caught herself. She had not said 'babe' for years. Not since…Bobby… She laid her head back and thought about how fast things were moving.

"Slow down Amanda, you are going to scare him off!" she said in a stern voice inside of her head. Stefan continued to talk about the picture.

"I just thought that would be a cool picture to start our trip together. I should have taken a picture of the car loaded up, or you standing in the lobby, Amanda," Stefan said with a smile.

"You're a Dork." Amanda meant it as a playful way of saying "aw—that is *so sweet*."

Stefan reached over and squeezed her hand.

Amanda felt her eyes fill with tears, where did this man come from? Was this something God had planned for years? She was at a loss to answer, she just smiled. Amanda was in love with nature, "the art work of God." She could appreciate the structure and beauty of buildings but felt man had no master plan when it came to their location and impact, although, the Inca's seemed to get it. She was amazed with their choice of locations and the way they built their buildings, with the stars and earth in mind.

"Have you ever been to Peru or Stonehenge?" Amanda asked.

"No, but it sounds like that would be an awesome place to visit. We could see design, art and functionality all in the same place. It should be our first trip after the building is built. We will take a month off and travel. Hell, we can take off for two months, if you can get away." Stefan replied as he ran his finger back and forth on her leg, thinking how natural this all seemed.

Amanda smiled. Again, from ear to ear, she smiled.

Looking out the window she began to daydream. The city was gone and as far as you could see, it was God's country. She was on a trip with a man who made her heart beat fast. His kiss was deeper and with more passion than anyone before, and she knew her desire for him was more than physical. She *liked* him...truly *liked* him.

Though Amanda was dressed in hiking pants…they were still tight, like stockings with pockets sewn on. She was just inches away as he reached down to adjust the volume of the music. He glanced in her direction—down to the knee her legs were perfectly shaped. She was a painting of beauty...a post card, a poster child for the designer to sell the hiking pants to the world.

How incredibly beautiful, Stefan thought to himself..."Wow"

Stefan found himself looking longer than he thought he should have. Awkwardly, he quickly looked away. His heart was racing. He thought to himself. "I'm acting like a kid in high school. I can't believe this is happening to me."

Stefan asked Amanda, "How did you get involved in the environment?"

This was a first for Amanda. Most men were not interested in her desires or passions. Even men in her industry were more interested in her body than the fact that something mattered to her. She was more than willing to share her feelings with a man who really wanted to hear them; even more willing to share her dreams with a man who could potentially be a part of them.

Amanda found herself smiling more and more as the day slipped on. Every once in a while something was said that brought her to tears...not of sorrow, but laughter. She could not remember the last time a man truly made her laugh. Laughter is a powerful thing. It can cause the kinetic energy between two people to spark—and spark, it did.

While Amanda was a talker, Stefan was more reserved and shy. He was not a social person. He was more laid back, and he thought before he spoke. His friends were based on the quality of conversation more than the bond of social fulfillment.

Stefan did not like talking about his past, and was reluctant to talk about his childhood. He did not feel there was value in talking about the past or what feelings really meant. He felt out of place. He told her he never truly dated. He explained that he had avoided serious relationships. His studies took most of his time and thoughts, along with his drive to create the perfect building. His mind was previously occupied, never given the time to feel.

Amanda wasn't scared. If anything, she was sad for him. Amanda had been in a serious relationship, but the young man died. So, she knew what it was like to fall in love with someone. She knew what it was like to be close. She knew what it was like to loose love.

Here beside her, was a man who had never experienced the touch of a woman in an intimate way. She knew that he had sex, but there is a difference in sex and intimacy. Loving someone and touching someone were, truly two different things. Her eyes started to fill with tears as he explained his story, the surface of his life.

She was very intuitive, and she knew words spoken unsolicited often told you more about a person than any answer to a question asked. Sometimes, listening was the answer. She could tell that Stefan lived a lonely life. He had built up walls so high he that he could not see the true beauty of life

THREE HOURS IN

"Hey—Plymouth, New Hampshire is just a few miles ahead." Stefan said.

"Wow, time sure is flying," Amanda replied, looking at the time on the radio. It had been three hours, but it seemed like they just left.

"Do you come out here often?"

Stefan replied, "No, I have never been this way, I am usually forced to stay around cities, they seem to be the only ones that can afford to build the projects I draw."

"Well, start building smaller buildings!"

They both looked at each other and laughed. Stefan was always in cities, subways and man-made objects. He never ventured out beyond the cities. Though he loved the buildings he never wanted his structures to intrude on the emotional well-being of a city, or to oppose its energy instead of expand it. He wanted people to be amazed when they saw his work from a distance. He wanted his buildings to make people want to come to the city from all over the place.

A beacon in the distance; a spotlight, if you will. That was his goal for all of his projects, a place where the mind could rest, spiritually. It was like Stefan was a poet, yet, instead of words; he used metal, glass, and stucco to touch the heart and soul.

Stefan's was an old soul, according to his grandmother. She said that he was from Rome, maybe because she knew he loved the Coliseum, and Roman architecture. Or maybe she truly believed he was an old soul.

Stefan pulled off onto the exit for Plymouth. It was time to stretch their legs and gas up before they reached the cabin. It was a chance for Stefan to look at Amanda without worrying about a curve on the mountain road or a deer running out in front of them. While Stefan filled the S.U.V. with gas, Amanda went inside to get something to drink. As she headed back to the S.U.V., she stopped half way to take a drink of water. Stefan happened to turn as she was tilting the bottle of water to her lips for a sip. He was frozen in time; the sun was behind her causing a golden glow around her body. He stood there looking at her, he was moved by her beauty. Her hair was blowing in the breeze, and her shirt pressed against her like spilled milk against her body, the out-line of her bra painted on the skin only to keep the eyes in check. Stefan stood there, forgetting the very reason he got out of his car.

"You are truly beautiful, Amanda... really, you are."

She blushed and slowly swayed back and forth. Her body desperately wanted him to touch her and to kiss her like yesterday.

He told her..."Move to the right... Over by the fence..."

"Just a little... more... there, that's it."

"Hold it... right there—got it."

"Wow" Amanda said as she looked at the photograph...you are really good, I am impressed."

He smiled and took her hand... "We better get going."

They walked to the SUV, and he opened her door. She stood there for a moment hoping he would kiss her like he did after their lunch date. Her eyes were screaming, "Take me!"

But, Stefan told her, "Get in, we need to get going."

She sat down disappointed. Almost pouting she reached for her seat belt, as she pulled it across her breasts she felt his lips touching hers. He kissed her deeply and passionately. His right hands slide across her left breast. Her body tensed as she moaned. He held the side of her breast, gently, with feeling. He slowly reached up and held both sides of her face, and kissed her. Their lips were hot and their hearts pounded. Amanda was getting light headed, not from lack of air but the heat of her body.

Stefan said, "Wow!"

He looked deep in her eyes... "Damn girl, you are so incredibly hot!" Stefan walked back to the driver's side of the car.

Amanda noticed that a button had come undone on her shirt exposing the purple laced bra. She started to button it back but decided to let Stefan suffer the rest of the way there. Every time he looked in her direction he would see the side of her bosom.

As for Stefan, he was in heat, love, anything but lust... he had no desire to have sex, and in fact he was happy just being able to touch her. He was in heaven; this was the best trip of his life.

They got back on the main road and headed north. The elevation gradually changed from rolling hills to small mountains. Around and up, the mountain roads curved through passes that once were used by horsemen and wagons. Stefan found himself starting to actually look around, he was enjoying the scenery. He saw how the tree line followed the river, how the mountains extended up into the heavens. Every once in a while Amanda would say...

"Wow look at that..."

Stefan would turn his head, and much to his surprise, he found beauty in the landscape. Objects that he had seen all his life, but never took the time to truly appreciate. Everywhere he looked God had built mountains, rivers, trees all with rough and smooth textures. So many beautiful colors, everywhere he looked, he saw creation in a totally different light.

"We are only about an hour away," Amanda said, as she placed her hand on his leg.

Stefan tensed. He was not ready for her to touch his leg. Men are ok with their arms and shoulders being touched, but when a woman touches the leg that sends electricity up the body. He had not felt that tingle in a long time, the warm soft touch of a woman's hand.

"Are you hungry? Do you want to stop and get something to eat?"

Amanda replied, "There is a restaurant about twenty miles up on the right. Let's stop there."

They pulled up in front of the restaurant. It was a small, rustic looking building next to a river. The sign read, "Momma's Place."

Stefan said, "its official, I am taken' you to Momma's Place."

They both started laughing. Amanda was feeling desires that she had not felt in a long time, she needed to express them. As they walked towards the front door, Amanda rubbed Stefan's back, leaned over and kissed the side of his face.

Stefan smiled, "Thank you."

Two metal chickens sat on each side of the door. On the right side of the porch was a blue tick hound. He looked like a piece of art, until he raised his head and looked in their direction. Amanda knelt down next to him and started petting his head. Such a sad looking dog, she thought as he laid his head back down between his paws, like he was giving up on ever getting to go anywhere but the porch.

Stefan just smiled. Stefan had been so busy in life, he had forgotten about the real world. Places where families still sat around a table for supper, where tractors were parked in the yard not for show but because they were a part of daily life.

A blue tick hound and a beautiful woman smiling at him was definitely a different side of life than he had ever seen before. Amanda told the old dog how handsome he was. Her voice was sweet and soft, filled with concern and compassion. The old hound just sighed.

They made their way inside, and Amanda saw the restroom and told Stefan to hang on for a second so she could wash her hands. She was only gone a minute, and Stefan waited for her in the foyer. He was not hard to find. He was the only man without a plaid shirt or overalls. The table had an incredible view of the river. Stefan pulled out her chair, as she sat down. He then, headed off to the men's room to wash his hands as well.

Standing there in front of the sink, he looked into the mirror and said, "Wow she is something else. Don't blow it, Stefan...don't blow it."

A lot of men like the candle of excitement. They don't care if it's dark again. From one heart beat to the next, it does not matter as long as they get that feeling. Stefan was incapable of that. He was intense and passionate.

In the past, when he found himself liking a woman, Stefan would find faults to distract him. But with Amanda, he had taken down the walls. Now, his biggest fear was that he would run her off by being too passionate, too kind. Stefan had very bad experiences with women. So, his way of protecting himself was to dive into his work; make *it* his passion. He stayed away from women, and he made it so there was never time to date. This way, he avoided the pain and heartache that always seems to follow a relationship.

Amanda was different. Stefan quickly dried his hands and headed towards the table. Amanda was sitting down by a window that looked out at the river. He stopped, his heart was racing. Without even thinking he reached into his pocket and got out his phone and took a picture. The second picture of their journey. Amanda was looking out the window as she heard the clicking of the camera. She turned and smiled. Stefan took another picture.

It was the perfect setting for the woman of his dreams, Stefan was in heaven.

"You are so beautiful...so incredibly beautiful."

It slipped out; he didn't mean to say it out loud. How could he not tell her how he felt? Amanda blushed squeezing her hands together beneath her chin, like an answered prayer.

She said, "Thank you Stefan…you are something yourself."

Stefan sat down and took in the amazing view. He saw a river winding from high in the mountains, making its way, zigzagging through openings to find its self in front of the restaurant. A picture-like setting outside the window, you could not dream of a better location for a country restaurant.

Stefan thought about all the expensive restaurants with a view of buildings or crowded streets; how people had to book reservations hours or days in advance, just to get a table. His mind was working…he never stopped thinking… "What if I designed the building as a plateau layered like a rock facing the northern view across from The Falls, and the eastern view at an incline so people could not look down but only see the skyline and the setting sun." Stefan smiled…this trip was already inspirational. It touched his heart and mind.

Amanda asked, "What are you thinking about? You're smiling."

Stefan looked at Amanda. The sun sparkled in her eyes.

"Heaven, I am looking at heaven and it makes me smile."

Amanda had never known a man who spoke honestly with her. There were those who would flirt and try to get into her pants, yes, but not pure honesty. She was moved by the words. He was poetic without meaning to be; charming with no selfish thought, and he was making her heart beat out of control.

Stefan had been so busy in life that he thought the only thing that would bring him excitement was a new building. The texture, the lines, glass and steel sitting on a concrete field. He had never really taken the time to look at the earth, the very thing that made his world possible. Amanda brought him to a different place inside his heart and soul. Just her smile caused his body to ache to be near her, and to hold her in his arms.

Imagine a painter living in a room full of paint brushes. For an architect, living in a city was just like that. Everything that he loved was around him. Stefan never took the time to look at the rest of the world. This was new for him. He had no idea. Nature was a canvas created by God. The ultimate architect. He used lines and shapes, colors and textures. Amanda helped Stefan open his eyes. Stefan was truly happy.

Looking at the menu, he started to smile. He read the menu out loud: "cornbread, collard greens, chitterlings, squirrel, quail, fried chicken, duck and catfish," just to name a few... He lowered the menu and made eye contact with Amanda, they were both caught up in the beauty of the eyes, the way a face wrinkles a little when you smile.

They were in love, both knowing it, but neither one able to say it out loud yet.

"This is real food. You won't find this beneath golden arches. I bet they don't have wine here. Moonshine maybe, but not wine." Stefan said in a soft voice.

"You really have lived a sheltered life Stefan."

"Sadly I live where I create my work. I have never ventured out."

They enjoyed lunch. Stefan had foods that he had never eaten before, in a setting that was right out of a country magazine.

Stefan asked Amanda, "Tell me more about where we are going."

"We are going to my favorite spot in the whole world, a mountain top called Eagle's Nest. The name came from the fact that it is so high above the tree line, a place where eagles fly. It takes about two hours to climb to the rock face," Amanda replied like a seasoned guide.

Stefan was afraid of heights, but he figured they would be on solid ground. So, it is just an elevation of land. Not a building made by man. He silently convinced himself he could handle it.

Amanda continued, "I go there two or three times a year. It is the place I find myself, to make sure that I am following the path God wants me to follow."

Stefan looked at her. He was a religious man. He attended catholic schools, and knew there was a higher power, but he questioned whether he truly believed. He was skeptical. All the terrible things in life, all the suffering…Stefan could not imagine God allowing children to suffer.

"Sometimes it is hard to believe that God would allow bad things to happen," Stefan said.

"Stefan, God does not allow things to happen. He simply allows life to happen."

"What are you saying?"

"Well, it is one thing to create a work of art, but it is up to the work of art to exist. We are given the ability to talk as children, right? Well, we choose what we say by process of thought. God gave us the ability to speak but, we choose what we say. Is it Gods fault that we say something mean, or lie? No. Is it Gods fault that the brain does not work and we lose speech? If you build your building and the screws fail, is it your fault or even the plywood's fault that the screws failed?"

Stefan's brain was working hard, taking in all she had to say.

People explain the why, but it has always has been a question to him. She made a good point. Several good points. I am not sure if it was the fact that he now had reason to question his doubt or if he just wanted to avoid a philosophical conversation with such a beautiful view, so he changed the subject as he squeezed her hand.

"Amanda, what is the plan for the rest of the day?"

Stefan was used to being in charge. He was responsible for projects that could have as many as two hundred people. Everything thing in his life was detail oriented, so for him to not have a plan, for him to not be in charge, was strange.

Amanda replied, "I figure we will go to the cabin first and drop off the gear, and then we will do a sunset hike near Mount Moosilauke. There is a rock face there, and when you climb it, you can see the setting sun twice, it is really cool! It twists and turns, at one point your view is blocked by ridges. Though the sun has not truly gone down, you end up hiking in near darkness until you reach the top of the ridge and. There it is! So magical and beautiful."

As Amanda was describing the view, Stefan could not help but think how beautiful she was. He was moved by her passion for life and the beauty of the earth.

"I want you to know that I am having the time of my life," Stefan told her as he placed the tip on the table.

Stefan always tipped more than the norm. Even when the waiter was not that good but tried hard or was overworked, Stefan always left a large tip. Many times he would go to the manager after the meal just to share how good a job the waiter did. He knew that life was not fair to everyone. It was his way of giving to those who worked hard.

Finally on the road again, they listened to classical music as the trees went by like grass along the road. Time seemed to go by faster than before.

"There, over there, that's it. Turn at that gate up there on the right."

Stefan pulled in slowly, it was an old road which wound up the mountainside, and there was a small clearing on each side.

"You are going to be amazed at the view, Stefan!"

Amanda told him, smiling; clearly excited.

The cabin was a beautiful old log cabin, with a large walk-around porch. As Amanda took him through the house, he could feel the relaxing energy, the calm of the home. It was peaceful, tranquil and relaxing. When they walked out onto the back porch, Stefan was at a loss for words.

As far as he could see, there were edges of mountains. In all directions, there were green trees and lakes like drops of water sparkling in the sun. His soul smiled. He noticed how everything belonged in its space, how the lines were clear, the colors complimented each other, and he was moved.

"Wow, Amanda. You're right. This is amazing!"

He pointed to a rock formation that stood out off to the north. "That is beautiful. What is that one called?"

Amanda proudly told him, "That is Eagle's Nest, look, see how it sticks out above the trees, just like a nest?" They stood there looking out over the trees, but time was not stopping.

"We need to get going. Let's get dressed. There is a guest room down that hall."

Amanda was anxious to get to the trail. They dressed in separate rooms and then gathered the gear they needed and headed for the SUV.

"Are you ready to touch the hand of God?"

Stefan looked at her and smiled. In a way he believed her, that she had the ability to touch the hand of God.

"It's only because you are an angel, Amanda."

They both looked at each other, lost in a moment of sincerity, lost in the power of the electricity of standing next to someone that makes your heart beat so hard you can hear it. Amanda looked away. She was afraid that he would see how much she wanted him. How much she wanted to hold him. The energy between them was building like a stream heading to a raging river. They headed north towards Eagle's Nest but they were only going about ten miles to Hickory Falls.

Hickory Falls was named after all the trees along the river leading up to the water fall. Stefan noticed when he opened the door he could hear the water falling from the top of the mountain. "It is loud, I cannot even see it, yet I can hear it."

Amanda smiled and rubbed her hand on his back. "You poor, sheltered man."

Again, this was something he had never experienced.

Amanda was tightening her boots. Stefan looked at the lines of her body, the way her back was arched, and her bottom curved into the shape of the letter C.

She turned in his direction and said, "Tighten your strings. Loose boots can cause you to break an ankle."

He knelt down and reached into his pocket, taking out the camera he took another picture of Amanda. She was starting to become a fashion model. Every time she heard the clicking of the camera her heart beat faster. She turned to find the camera, not for attention, but because she knew Stefan was there. In only a few short days, a man longed to take pictures of her, tell her she was beautiful, and smiled when he was next to her, she was in heaven.

Stefan had a plan for the photographs. He was going to blow up the pictures and put them on the walls of his home... maybe their home, one day.

"Good thing you don't have to pay for film, in the olden days if you took pictures you had to buy film. Usually 24 or 36 exposures, and then you still had to take them to a lab and have them developed. Today, it is a different world...everything is instant," Amanda said.

The closer to the waterfall they got, the louder the noise, similar to the sound of a freight train. Imagine the sound of running water, but a hundred times louder. It was an amazing site, thousands of gallons of water falling one hundred and fifty feet into a black pool.

They made it to the base. There were a few other people standing around. Stefan asked an old man if he would mind taking a picture of them together. Amanda was so happy. Here was a man that wanted to be with her and do things that she wanted to do.

The old man took the picture, then said "Wait, one more...this time kiss the bride."

Stefan's heart beat erratically. They looked at each other and kissed. It lasted for a moment, maybe several, they did not remember.

The only thing that stopped the embrace was the old man yelling, "Got it...I got it."

Looking at each other, they were frozen in happiness.

"Let's go," Amanda said.

"Tomorrow, we will come back here and go swimming," Amanda said with a smile. The first thing that came to Stefan's mind was not whether the water was cold, but what would she be wearing? You see, clearly he was attracted to her, he already had imagined touching her body. So, the thought of swimming next to her in the water, made his heart race. He found himself blushing, lost in his thoughts.

He told her, "That's a great idea. I look forward to that."

"We are going to go to the left of the waterfall and head up into that pass. Before we reach the top, the sun will have already set. Once we reach the top, we will be able to see the sun set again. It should take us about an hour to get to the top of this rock ledge, so today's climb will only be about two hours." Amanda sounded like a guide.

"I don't want you to do too much too soon; tomorrow we will climb that mountain over there. That is Eagle's Nest."

Stefan looked across the forest in the distance. A rock face stuck out above the trees, some 300 feet.

"That is like climbing a 30 story building, and then some." Stefan said almost nervously.

"Stefan, this is my world. I've been climbing these mountains since I was a child, and you have to trust me. I have to trust you when I am riding in your elevators, or standing on the 40th

floor. Have a little faith. Everything is going to be fine."
Amanda's voice was assuring and confident.

"We can trust that God built the mountains better than any
building a man could have constructed...I've been there 100
times. You can trust me, just like I trust you."

Stefan smiled; he was putting his trust in a woman he barely
knew. Stefan knew nothing about bears, mountain lions or
wolves. All he knew about the wilderness was that it was a
dangerous place. Not only were there things that could harm
you out there, but you could get lost. Stefan immediately
started thinking of *Peter and the Wolf.*

He got nervous. "Amanda, what about the wildlife? Things
like um...wolves?"

Amanda started laughing. "Stefan, there's nothing to worry
about. I have been hiking in these mountains all my life. I am
aware of the dangers around here, as well as how to avoid
them."

Amanda didn't slow down. Stefan had to keep moving to keep
up. It was as if she knew that he would choose to either follow
or go back to the car. So they made their way up the path.
Much of the climb was steep. Stefan often had to reach for
small trees to pull him up, like hiking sticks.

Many times, people look at a sport as something easy to accomplish. However, people often forget there's a skill set required to achieve the goal, which takes a long period of time to learn. If one has never hiked an incline, it is very difficult to lean forward, maintain balance, and walk at a normal pace.

Although Stefan was an athlete, he still had trouble keeping up with Amanda. In a way, this intrigued him more. Amanda could tell Stefan was struggling a bit, so she sat down and waited for him to catch up.

"Do you need to take a break?" She asked.

"I really do need a break. I think I just need to drink a little water. Maybe my muscles are not quite stretched out enough." Stefan was admitting that climbing was not a simple sport.

Amanda smiled, "Right, I'm sure that's what it is. Once you take a drink, I'm sure that the throbbing in your legs will go away."

They both looked at each other and started laughing. Stefan felt he had met his match. Here was a woman that was beautiful and driven.

"So the city boy can't hack hiking with a country girl?"

"No… that's not it. That's not it at all. I haven't had anything to drink, and it's been a week or two since I've been in the gym. My body's not used to this much exertion in such a short period of time. Plus you have to consider the fact that I am not used to the altitude." I sounded good to Stefan.

Then he broke down and smiled. "Okay you're kicking my ass!" They both laughed.

As Stefan drank his water, he noticed the rocks sticking out of the ground, and how the roots of the trees twisted and turned. Nothing was out of place. It seemed that everything was intertwined. Stefan was truly amazed. He never took the time to realize that the wilderness was so complex. He always considered it a random thing. Looking down from airplanes, it just seemed like fields of green. This was the first time the wilderness was personal. He studied it, just as he studied the buildings around him—a formula used by God that clearly worked.

He reached over, signaled for Amanda's attention, and pointed to a root system that had grown into the side of a rock face to support the growth of a tree. In a place where nothing should have grown, a beautiful tree rose 15 feet into the sky. He looked at Amanda. She looked back at him and smiled.

Stefan was experiencing feelings he had never felt before, seeing things he had always ignored. He took out his camera and captured a photograph of the trees.

Amanda looked at him and saw how pleased he was. She was moved because he was now seeing her world through her eyes.

"Stefan, we better get moving or we will miss the sunset."

He was like a child being rushed at the zoo. He stuck his phone back in his pocket and rushed to catch up with her. Stefan saw Amanda's world as a beautiful place where man was a visitor. Soon Stefan was going to see what drove Amanda every day to make phone calls and lobby for the wilderness.

As they went around the boulder, Amanda stopped and leaned against a tree looking down at the ground. There was a six-pack of beer—not aluminum cans—but glass. Three empty bottles, one bottle laying in the holder and two broken ones against the rocks. Amanda wanted to see what Stefan would say.

Stefan was a few feet behind her and as he approached he asked, "What are we stopping for?"

Amanda said, "I just wanted to take a break for second…"

Then Stefan said in the disgusted voice, "Really?"

Amanda was shocked at the tone of his voice. It caught her off guard for a second. She thought he was mad at her, but was pleasantly surprised when Stefan continued his comment, "Are people so selfish, so disrespectful, that they would leave trash in a place like this? Why would those people even come up here?"

Amanda smiled. Deep inside, she realized that this man cared. Stefan had never marched in protest; he never found time to stand up for a cause, but for the first time in his life, he felt righteous anger. For the first time in his life he understood that the wilderness was innocent.

He went over to the bottles and put them back into the card board holder, and he picked up the broken glass. He reached into his backpack, took out a t-shirt, and wrapped it around the empty bottles, keeping any glass from spilling, and then he stuck that in his backpack. He didn't do it to impress Amanda. He did it because he truly felt bad that people would be so rude and un-thoughtful.

Neither one said a word, but at that moment, Amanda's heart realized that she had fallen in love with this man. She found herself falling for a man who created marvelous structures and had a genuine, loving, and compassionate heart. She felt like a bride standing at the end of the walkway, and her heart was overflowing with emotions.

The question in her mind, the biggest concern regarding Stefan, was just answered. Not only did he react to the ignorance of humankind, but also, he took on the burden of carrying the broken glass down the mountain. Amanda had never been with a man that cared enough to pick up the bottles. She truly was in love.

"Now you see why I fight to keep the wilderness clean. You know, Stefan, it does not take too many people like this and soon there would be broken glass everywhere."

"Amanda, now I see this side of you. I did not understand until now. I see why you choose to fight for the wilderness. You've shown me a side of life that I never considered. You are an amazing woman."

Stefan leaned down and kissed her cheek.

They did not exchange anymore words. She didn't tell him to hurry up, or catch up. She just turned and moved up the mountain again. Stefan thought to himself that following Amanda was not a terrible thing. He could watch the muscles in her legs flex, the curves of her body constantly moving side to side. He was having the time of his life, with the love of his life. He was learning more about himself than he ever thought he knew.

It was almost dark, and Stefan was actually a little bit nervous, because everything he learned in school was about pioneering men, not women. There were no stories about women like Amanda. It seemed that all great tales ended with a knife and a grizzly bear. Somehow, Stefan didn't think it would be a fair fight between Amanda and a grizzly bear. So in a way, Stefan was kind of scared, but he had faith in her, and he trusted her.

She turned around and whispered, "We're almost there, you doing okay?"

"I'm right behind you Babe."

Amanda smiled. She loved the sound of him calling her Babe. Maybe it was because they were in the wilderness or the kisses from earlier in the day. It really didn't matter why he was calling her Babe, it just made her smile. For the next 30 or 40 yards, she could not get the smile off her face. She was afraid to turn around because she didn't want Stefan to see the way she was smiling.

As they made their way to the top, Stefan noticed there was a gold light coming from the top of the trees. It was as if they were walking into a building and the door was open; someone was standing in the doorway with a giant golden flashlight. It was the most amazing view Stefan had ever seen. He was speechless as they cleared the trees and made their way out onto the rock face. Just as Amanda had described, he watched the sun set for the second time. Stefan could see in all directions. The forest was beneath their feet, and in the distance, the orange ball was sinking into the edge of the earth.

Stefan turned to Amanda, "I never thought I would see the sun set twice in one day."

He wrapped his arms around her. As she laid her head against his chest, they watched the sun set together. He felt he was as close to Heaven as he would ever be. He had fallen in love with the perfect woman. He chased happiness all his life but never found it. Now God brought this woman into his life at the point when he had stopped looking.

Amanda turned to Stefan, "Do you see why I am in love with the wilderness? Can you see why I believe in God? Stefan you're an architect, do you really think all this just happened by mistake? "

Stefan pulled her tight against him and kissed the side of her face. He didn't say a word not because he didn't want to answer, but he was lost in the moment…lost in her beauty. For the first time in his life, he was not in a rush to go anywhere.

He had no plans that were pressing. In fact, he didn't even know if his cell phone was on or off. He was genuinely happy.

Amanda continued to talk about God. She was a strong Christian, not just based on the Bible, but because of the example her father set for her.

"Stefan, you know that everything is based on mathematics, formulas, and cell structure. When we can look around and see how perfect everything is, how can someone not believe in God? I question things, and I don't have the answer to many of my questions, but I can tell you that when I stand on top of the world I have no doubt that the ultimate architect is God."

Stefan was moved. Not only was this woman devoted to protecting the wilderness, but she also stood for her principals and her beliefs. She made him look at his own life and caused him to consider the strength of his own beliefs.

Amanda closed her eyes and rested her head against his chest again in silence. Even the clouds moved slowly as the sunset disappeared. His heart beat against her back. Amanda slowly turned around and leaned up. With lips soft and ready Stefan was already halfway there...they kissed.

They kissed at the top of the world. The energy between them was electric. Amanda's body tingled and Stefan's heart beat strong against her breasts. It was a long, sensual kiss. There was no fondling. No hands searching for areas they've never been. He just held her softly and kissed her deeply. She took a deep breath and leaned back placing her hands on his chest.

"Stefan, we need to head back down. It's getting late and we really shouldn't be up here too long in the night."

Stefan raised an eyebrow and said, "Are we in danger? I mean, it's a good hour back to the car. Are we okay?" She laughed out-loud.

"I'm just saying, Stefan, as the cool air comes down, the rock face gets slippery and we really shouldn't be here too long after dark because the rocks can be very dangerous. It is safer climbing in the middle of the day."

A relieved smile came over his face. Stefan said "I'm right behind you,"

She didn't totally understand why he smiled, or what he meant. He had the pleasure of watching her bottom move up and down all the way up the mountain and now after kissing her deeply and warmly, he was going to watch her shake it all the way down. Stefan was elated. He knew this weekend could never be replaced. He felt in his heart that this was the woman for him. He had never felt this way before.

"Show the way, Babe. I'm right behind you."

Again, Amanda couldn't get over the term 'Babe.' She was so very happy. But this time she turned around and told Stefan, "Catch me if you can?"

It was almost like a cat and mouse game. She didn't speed up though. She kept the same pace, because she knew that descending from a mountain in the evening hour wasn't a safe thing to do if you weren't experienced. She knew that her wits had to be about her because they were in mountain lion country, and the wolves did run in packs. So, her experience as a climber and naturalist kept her sharp, and prepared for anything that might cause them harm.

It took a little longer to climb down the mountain then it took them to hike up. They made it back to the SUV. Stefan was panting, not from intimacy exchanged, but from the long hike. Amanda found herself thinking of Stefan sexually. What it must feel like to touch him, run her hands across his bare chest. As they drove down the road towards the direction of the cabin, Stefan reached over and put his hand on her leg.

Amanda stuck her finger in the corner of her mouth and looked out the window. She wanted to scream, exuberantly. She wanted to tell him how turned on she was.

But she kept it inside. She just smiled and put her hand on top of his and asked him if he'd had a good time.

"It was amazing, Amanda. I've never experienced anything like that before. I can't wait until tomorrow. You are one amazing woman."

Amanda fought back the tears. Bobby was the last man to call her amazing. The only other man that had ever said anything to her like that was her father. Stefan telling her she was beautiful and amazing, made her heart race. Walls were coming down that had been up for years.

"Well, you're going to need to get some sleep tonight, buddy. Tomorrow we're hiking twice as far, and to a much higher altitude."

Stefan smiled and said, "Bring it on! I'll build us a bridge if we need to cross troubled waters!"

He caught Amanda off guard and then she started laughing, "I'll bet you would."

"I would Amanda. I would build you a bridge and carry you across it!"

They smiled at each other and for the next few miles they just rode hand in hand…his hand against her leg and her hand holding his hand there. They were both feeling the passion and excitement in the air. They weren't kids, but they were young enough to experience a true love, a feeling that could not be taken away.

THINGS GET HOTTER

They arrived at the cabin. They were both exhausted, but the sexual tension was growing like the winds before the storm.

Amanda said, "I'm going to go take a shower."

Stefan replied, "I'll go get cleaned up as well."

Amanda walked into the bathroom and closed the door. Secretly, she was wishing that Stefan was still following her. As she took off her clothes and climbed into the shower, with the warm water rinsing her skin, she could think of nothing but Stefan. She imagined his hands on her, pushing her against the cold tile. She was in love. Some people would say lust, but she knew it wasn't lust.

For years Amanda had plenty of men hitting on her, plenty of men who have offered her the moon. Men who looked like models, but Amanda was not about that. She couldn't kiss a man unless she felt something, and she certainly couldn't let a man touch her, unless she was truly willing to give herself to him. Nevertheless, she had a craving that was burning inside of her to be with Stefan, to allow him to touch her and to kiss her, again. Over and over.

She took a long shower, mostly to cool her body temperature, to compose herself, and try to keep from throwing herself at him. She put on what she would call pajamas, which was her cotton sweat pants with red checkers, and a white long-john shirt, thick enough so if it got cold, he wouldn't notice her nipples.

She brushed her hair and looked in the mirror, but still, all she could think about was Stefan behind her, his hands on her body, kissing her neck and holding her close. She slammed the brush down on the counter, trying to put the thought of making love to him out of her mind. But the sexual frustration was slowly building. She was afraid that she was going to make the first move.

She whispered, "Boy I am in trouble."

She made her way back to the kitchen and found the vegetables. Stefan still had not returned from the guest room. So, she started cutting up the vegetables: mushrooms and lettuce.

Stefan was facing his own emotions down the hall. He, too, could not stop thinking about Amanda. Taking off his shirt only made him think about taking off hers. And when his pants dropped to the ground, he thought about her hips and what it would be like to slide her pants down the sides of her hips, slowly. He pictured her perfect shape that he had watched all day go up and down the mountain. He thought about holding her as the sun set, and the kiss that was remarkable.

Stefan wasn't immune to feelings. He didn't have a deficiency that caused him not to long for the touch of a woman. He'd just chosen all these years to stay away from problems, to avoid emotions that would only lead to pain. He felt that she was the one. He so desperately wanted to be with her, hold her, and feel her heart beat against his chest. He already made love to her in his mind over and over again, but it wasn't real yet. He had not exchanged whispered words, or the felt her naked, against him, but it was all he could do not to think about it. He knew that he longed for her.

As he stood there, drying off and putting on his boxer briefs and a pair of dark blue pajama bottoms with a Calvin Klein silk top shirt, he looked in the mirror and said,

"Here we go."

As he made his way back to the kitchen, he saw her standing there, with her wet hair. He paused to take in the sight of her in the long-john shirt and plaid bottom pants.

He stopped and leaned against the wall, took a deep breath and said, "Wow. You are absolutely stunning."

Amanda felt it inside. It was as if he whispered it in her ear, holding her against the wall. She leaned forward and tensed.

Without even looking in his direction, she said, "You're just saying that."

"No, I mean it. You are the most amazing woman I have ever seen."

As he walked towards her, Amanda dropped the knife into the sink and it made a loud sound. As she turned around, he was already upon her. He took her in his arms, put his hand on the side of her neck, and kissed her deeply. Her lips begged for him.

He couldn't help himself. He thought how the plan to sit next to her by the fire had changed; he couldn't even make it that far. Just seeing her in her pajamas, seeing her in the long-john shirt and the shape of her breasts...the hour-glass figure was too much. He had to kiss her again in the privacy of the cabin.

Amanda moaned as the temperature of their bodies rose. Again, and again they kissed. He could feel her nipples hard against his chest. He put one of his hands on her bottom and pulled her close. She knew that he was excited, knew that she had turned him on past the point of a casual kiss. But she also knew that she did not want to seem easy.

The struggle inside her was difficult, but she put her hands on his chest and pushed him back a little and said, "Let's eat supper. We've got plenty of time to talk."

Stefan smiled because she didn't say it meanly.

It was almost like saying, "We have plenty of time to make love later."

That's all Stefan heard. The word talk was just a synonym for, "Oh my gosh, I want to make love to you so badly," Stefan knew it.

He said, "Yeah, let's eat. I'm famished."

BOILING POINT

"What can I do? What do I you need help with? I see you've already started," Stefan said with a smile.

 It was almost as if they both tried to find something to occupy their desire. Stefan walked over and grabbed the tomatoes and started dicing them up. Amanda was working on the peppers, carrots, and mushrooms. The lettuce was already in a big bowl. They each took turns, almost like a rotation throwing the cut up vegetables into the bowl.

"This looks really good. Do you eat salad often?"

Amanda said, "I eat it all the time. Usually I have chicken or salmon, something like that with it, not just salad."

"Well, I can't say that I always eat that healthy but, you know, I don't eat a lot of junk food either. I mostly eat chicken, steak, and potatoes. I mean, basically I'm a guy."

Stefan chuckled and Amanda said, "That's okay. There's no problem in adjusting diets. I don't mind cooking steak and chicken for other people. I just... I'm not a big fan of eating it myself."

Stefan smiled because she was making a statement that there was going to be a future; that there was a possibility of them existing in the same residence in some way. Her making them supper was something that was possibly in their future.

Stefan said, "Sometimes change is good." And he affectionately put his hand on her bottom and patted. This pat was simply saying, oh, my gosh... I desperately want to touch that. She looked at him and smiled, "Kind of hard to cut with one hand... isn't it?"

From ear to ear, Stefan's grin was obvious, as he took his hand off her bottom and went back to cutting the tomatoes.

He said, "I'll tell you what, let me do what guys do and I'll go ahead and get a fire started."

"That's a good idea Stefan."

Even though it was autumn, it was 60 degrees out. The fire was more for the ambiance. It really wasn't necessary, but it was the whole experience of being out in nature and a desire to make her feel special. So, Stefan went ahead and built a fire. The whole time all he could think about was making love to Amanda.

By the time he finished, Amanda had the table set. She lit a single candle in the middle. The reflection sparkled in the wine, a red pinot noir, a soothing, soft flavor that melts on the lips. The salad was unique. There wasn't any meat, but it looked delicious. They sat down, not across from each other, but next to each other, and began to eat.

They talked less around the table than they did on the whole ride up, maybe because they were at a point now in the relationship that they both knew where it was going. They were no longer just two people interested in each other. Now, they were two people who longed for each other emotionally and physically. They didn't eat in a hurry. They took their time, almost as if to make the moment last longer.

Stefan reached over and put his hand on her leg. An electric pulse went through her body. She so wanted to push the salad bowls off the table and throw him on it, climb on top and make mad passionate love. But she controlled herself, and just looked at him and smiled. Her eyes were soft, and her lips were moist. Stefan knew by the way she was twitching her leg that her body clearly wanted his, It was only a matter of time before they both would lose control. In his past, this moment was planned and it seemed to follow a driven need. With Amanda, it was a pounding desire, a pulse so strong he could barely talk. He too, had thoughts of scattering salad bowls and hair being pulled. They looked at each other, both dreaming of moments to never be forgotten.

Do you wants some? Amanda asked.

Stefan froze because yes he did! He heard what he wanted to hear or at least what he wanted her request for more salad to be about. He knew that the slightest sign of submission to passion and he would spring like a lion on her. The room was quiet except the sound of the fire place and the fork sliding against the porcelain bowl.

"Amanda thank you for bringing me here, I can't believe that I got to see the sun set twice!"

It was amazing, wasn't it?" Amanda said.

"Just beautiful," Stefan said as he looked into her eyes. "You are just beautiful."

Amanda smiled.

OUT OF CONTROL

Stefan went to reach for his wine glass but he was mesmerized by her and he looked away too soon. His fingers just hit the edge of the glass, tipping it over, and splashing pinot noir all over her white long-john top. She jumped back, but as the cold red wine wet her breasts, seeping into her shirt.

Stefan said, "Oh Baby, I'm so sorry."

He took his napkin and started patting the wine on her breast— it was too much. The napkin slid out of his hand as he cupped her breasts and began to kiss her. The room was in a haze. The wine was cold against her breasts, and she longed for his touch, for his warm hands to hold them.

She moaned, as she kissed him deeply, and passionately. They stood up and embraced as the chairs squeaked across the wooden floor; it was as though they were two butterflies stuck together. They couldn't separate one without removing pieces of the other. Spinning in circles, they twirled slowly, while desperate moans echoed as their bodies became one.

They made their way over to the couch. Stefan laid her against the leather and climbed on top of her. Amanda pulled off her shirt. She had lost all sense of worry. She was already in too deep. Her body was aching for him, and at this point, her nakedness didn't matter. She knew that she wanted him. She knew that she wanted to give herself to him. Stefan knelt between her legs, as his eyes looked at the round breasts with dark nipples. He pulled off his shirt and tossed it over the side of the couch, onto the floor. He leaned down and passionately kissed her. Then he kissed her neck, working his way to her breasts, holding them gently and passionately. She ran her hands through his hair in confirmation of pleasure. He let his body press against hers. She could tell he was excited. He could feel her getting hotter. Deeply, he kissed, stopping only to whisper that she was beautiful into her ear.

Amanda ran her hands on each side of his rib cage. His muscles were defined. He had the means to go the gym twice a week. His body fat was only 8 percent. He was strong; his pecks were firm, followed by what women call a six pack, muscles that rolled on his stomach. She was having trouble breathing.

She reached down and untied his pajamas, sliding them off as he stood up. He reached down and hooked his thumbs on each side of her panties, beneath the pajama bottoms and quickly pulled them off and tossing them across the room. They were both naked, but neither one cared. He looked at her hips and the lines of her body. He was beyond excited. She lay back down as Stefan leaned between her legs and kissed her stomach and belly button. She gasped. She closed her eyes and bit her lip.

She tensed. She whispered, "Stefan...oh Stefan."

He made his way up her stomach, passed her breasts. Wrapping his arms around her back and on her shoulders, he pulled her body into his and she moaned. This wasn't a conquest, but an act of passion. He was not taking her. She was giving herself to him.

The temperature was hot. He kissed her deeply with great passion. Again and again, they moved back and forth on the leather. The fire crackled and popped. Her heartbeat raced and her eyes were soft. Stefan kissed the side of her neck as he held her tight into himself. She started to beg him not to stop as he whispered her name over and over.

They both collapsed, sweat running down the side of his face, and tears of joy and passion in her eyes. The tears of love only a woman feels. She was so in love with him, she could not stop whispering his name.

Amanda had never felt such passion, had never felt hands strong but gentle, had never had a man whisper that he loved her in her ear. Bobby and Amanda were in love but there was a lot about Bobby that Amanda had trouble with. He wasn't kind. He loved her but he wasn't gentle. He was self-absorbed. But, she was young and he had been the only guy that was allowed to touch her breasts, so it only seemed fitting that when he requested that they make love, it just seemed like an extension of what she'd already given him.

But with Stefan, she wanted him with every fiber of her being. With Stefan, it was about the way her heart felt and the way he felt against her. Amanda knew the first time she saw Stefan that they would make love. Call it instinct; call it a connection of energy. She had never thought that before. She had never seen a man before and said to herself, this is a man I want to make love to.

But with Stefan, it was the first thing that came to her mind. It wasn't about sex. It wasn't about the fulfillment. It was about giving, about sharing a soul with another human being and everything she'd imagined love should be. All the feelings she anticipated were real. Stefan took her by the hand and they walked to the shower. He held her around the waist as he turned the water on and adjusted the temperature. They stepped in. The steam started to rise to the ceiling.

A HOT SHOWER

The steam rose above their heads, collecting like a cloud. Visibility was limited but hands do not need to see when they search with passion. Their eyes closed, warm hands explored places private. Her lips trembled and her heart pounded. She was his every desire and he was her knight.

Even if words were whispered with passion, she could not hear, for her breathing was loud and her thoughts were fixed on the hands, lost in the pleasure they found. He was in love with her, she was his dream…the intimacy between them was greater than anything either had ever felt.

His hands were strong, but gentle. He was not afraid to pull her close, not afraid to make her beg. She was a prisoner of passion, desire and love. Even though they were in the privacy of their own home she felt as though they were at the base of the waterfall. With the world far away and nothing between them she felt like Eve making love to Adam.

There was an erotic pleasure in the way his hands felt on her body. Never before had a man touched her so softly, yet so deeply. Passion, like steam, sizzled between them; her eyes told the story. Her breasts against his chest caused electrical shocks to his body. Inches away, there was nothing to hide…and there were no regrets. With his tongue softly licking her ear, as her hands were pinned against the cold tile, she felt helpless. She wanted him again and again. His hands slid down her side slowly, rubbing her breasts then moving across her stomach.

She began to tremble; not from being cold, but from being too hot. She desperately wanted him to take her. With moans, she called to him, she slid her hand behind his neck, pulling him closer, hoping he would read the signals that were telling him that she was giving herself to him. Searching for many years Amanda knew that he was the one; there was something between them that had nothing to do with intimacy but passion. This man was better than all the men in her past combined, in just a short time he had her believing in love again. This is not a simple love or something on the surface, but true love.

Amanda searched for air to breathe, as she backed against the tile with her legs wrapped around him. She held his face and kissed him frantically. The water from the shower ran down like a waterfall.

She remembered thinking, this moment; this second; will never be forgotten. Even if they get married, even if they live 50 years, what she is feeling at this very moment could never be surpassed. No man had ever found a way to touch her inside, to make her shake for no reason, she was in heaven. Her body was made for his. She was feeling things that were beyond explanation.

"Stefan—please don't stop," she whispered into his ear.

Her voice was panicked, not from fear but from anticipation. They had been in the shower so long the water had turned cold, yet their bodies were so hot they did not notice. It was as if they were in a rage of passion, different from a rage of anger...

Stefan turned around and held her hands against the wall. Her body ached for his touch. He looked her in the eyes and told her he loved her. She was afraid to tell him that she loved him, but her moans came from the soul, a fulfillment of inner peace. Two people from two different worlds collided like a comet, and the outcome was sheer passion.

Like children playing with paint on a white wall, hand prints covered the glass door in all directions. The steam floated to the ceiling like a foggy morning on a black lake. They stood there and held each other tight...maybe in disbelief that they found each other, or maybe they were too scared to let each other go. Stefan turned the water off and opened the door. As the steam rolled out he reached for a towel and wrapped it around her naked body.

Amanda thought to herself... "Is this too good to be true?" All she could do was tell him how she felt. But how do I do that with a man I barely know, and yet with whom I was willing to be naked?

For many women, that is no problem. But for Amanda, letting a man see her naked was not something that she'd ever consider doing unless she was married. In fact the only man she'd ever been with was Bobby. That was six years ago, and Amanda had not been with a man since. She had gone out to dinner with a few guys, movies now and then, but she never let herself care about another man.

There was something about the time she spent with Stefan which caused her heart and soul to want more. He brought out the willingness to give herself to him, the desire to have the man that makes your heart beat, touch you intimately. To have his arms around you, be inside you... feel the pulse of his heartbeat is a feeling that can't be described, and Amanda so desperately wanted that. She had no regrets, as she watched Stefan dry his hair. The whole time he never took his eyes off her.

To Stefan, she was the perfect woman. She was compassionate. She viewed life as it was meant to be viewed. She had given Stefan an outlook that he had never had. She fulfilled dreams that he only thought happened in your sleep.

"I can't even see my face in the mirror. It's all your fault." Amanda said with a smile.

Even though they had planned on sleeping in separate rooms, the events of the night had changed everything, and Amanda didn't want Stefan more than a foot away from her. She wanted to be able to reach out and touch him in the night to make sure it was real. She wanted to be able to kiss him and tell him it wasn't a dream.

So, they slept in the same room, and for the first time in her life, she didn't move. She lay against him. When she and Bobby would spend the night together, she always got tired of the temperature and moved to her corner. But with Stefan it was different. With Stefan, it was as if she belonged against him. They were as one. There was a kindred spirit there that could not be shaken.

Amanda set the alarm, and they laid down next to each other sleeping peacefully. Occasionally, through the night, Stefan would wake up and give Amanda a kiss on the side of the cheek…on the forehead. Her naked body up against his, their temperature the same. She had finally found her soul mate, and Stefan his.

Before they knew it, the sun was rising and the alarm was ringing. Even though the very sight of Amanda made Stefan aroused, he knew the trip was about experiencing nature. He didn't want to take that time away from her. The wilderness was something she was so passionate about.

Amanda was nestled against Stefan as the sun began to shine through the trees. He began to kiss her softly, their hearts raced and their skin was warm. They both wanted to make love again, but Stefan knew they had other plans for the day and it was more important to set aside desire. As she leaned forward kissing, he slowly climbed out of bed and told her that he'd better go get ready.

"Wait, wait, wait. One more kiss. One more kiss" Amanda whispered.

Stefan's hand slipped through hers and said, "Don't worry, baby. We have tonight."

She smiled and pulled the silk sheets up around her breasts and took a deep sigh. So, it wasn't a dream. Stefan really did spend the night and they really did make love. She could smell him on her skin. She wrapped her arms around her as though he was hugging her and took a deep breath. She got dressed and went to the kitchen to make coffee.

Shortly, Stefan came out in his hiking attire looking like a professional hiker. She chuckled. She knew more about Stefan than she had ever known about any man in her life. She knew there was no way that he was going to go hiking unless he had the right outfit.

They poured their coffee and loaded their gear and headed out to the car. She wrapped her arms around his neck and gave him a long kiss and he smiled.

He said, "Amanda, I'm so in love with you, I don't know what to say. I don't know how to describe these feelings, but my heart feels like it's going to burst out of my chest."

She put her fingers on his lips and told him, "There's no need to talk. I feel the same way. Come on, let's get going."

Eagle's Nest was over an hour away. But first they were going to Hickory Falls to go swimming as she had promised. The hike to Eagle's Nest was much harder; twice as long as Hickory Falls. It was going to be a two hour hike to the summit. First they were going to spend some time at Hickory Falls and then grab a bite to eat before going to Eagle's Nest.

It was mid- morning when they arrived. She was wearing a polka dot bikini. She stripped out of her hiking gear and waded into the black water. Stefan started taking his clothes off as if he was trying to rescue her. Though he had made love to her, he still desperately wanted to be near her.

The water was cold; mountain streams are comprised of melted snow, water from deep inside the mountain rises to the surface. Since it's protected from the sun, it is typically very cold water. It was still morning, so there was steam rising off the water because of the contrast in temperature.

They waded out and embraced. Their kiss was hotter than the steam rising off the water. Their bodies caused more steam to rise, but Stefan didn't even notice how cold it was, or the goose-bumps on his arms, because he was in heaven. He was holding his dream, an incredible woman named Amanda.

Not really worried about time, they spent an hour just enjoying the waterfall. He held her in his arms while they moved around; talking about their feelings and the future they were planning. They were like two kids in high school…the innocence. There was no sexual intimacy this time. There was no fondling or touching.

They were just two people in love with each other, spending time together in an amazing place. The scenery behind them was better than any painting they had ever seen. They were truly in love. By the time they were ready to go, it was noon.

Amanda said, "Let's go get something to eat and then we'll head to Eagle's Nest."

It was one of the very first mountains Amanda ever climbed alone. One could say she found it by accident, but other climbers had been there before. Their names were written on the sides of the rocks, along with the year they were there. It was not a treacherous climb; an amateur could do it, but climbers had to be careful. Hikers needed to climb in the dry season, because the rocks' surfaces became like soap if they got wet. Like she told Stefan the day before, once the temperatures change, the rocks become slippery and it could become dangerous to climb. Stefan wasn't afraid, because he knew Amanda was not an amateur, she was a pro. She worked many rescue climbs and search parties in the past. He believed in her and he was in love with her.

They dried off and got dressed. They drove an hour and a half back to the restaurant where they had eaten the day before, and enjoyed a simple meal of catfish and sweet potatoes with cornbread. It was now 2:30 in the afternoon, a little later than Amanda had originally planned. Maybe it was because she was distracted by the passion they shared, but she didn't think about the weather changing.

Regardless, nothing was going to change their plans. It was a much higher altitude with a magnificent view that few people had seen, even in the middle of the day. She knew a route that was unknown to most climbers and it only had one section where you had to be careful. But, Stefan wasn't a clumsy person. He was an athlete, well built, and spent many hours in the gym, so she didn't worry about Stefan at all. And of course she never worried about herself she had been climbing all her life.

They reached Eagle's Nest and Stefan was in awe. He looked up and the rock face towered over the top of the trees. We're not talking about simple trees found in a park in Florida or New York. We're talking about trees that were 20 and 40 feet high. And yet they looked like toothpicks against the side of the face of the mountain. He could see the excitement in Amanda's face...she was home. She was back in the wilderness where she belonged.

But this trip home was not simply a trip she was taking alone. She had brought with her the man of her dreams. A man she had waited all her life to find and saved herself to share the special moments between a woman and a man. Stefan wasn't intimidated, but he was reminded that he was scared of heights. He followed Amanda as they made their way through the tall spruce up to the edge of the mountain that began to get more defined with rocks.

Amanda told him, "Always feel a rock before you put your foot down. Give it pressure and make sure it's stable. Don't ever assume that what looks to be stable is."

Stefan knew by the tone of her voice that she was serious. He knew that although she joked around about not worrying about danger, one false step and life would change forever.

They made their way across the south face. Much of the path was a 20 degree angle; steep enough to give you problems, but not so steep that you couldn't hold onto something. It wasn't like they were blindly climbing. Many mountain climbers before them had forged this path.

EAGLE'S NEST

It's unclear, why Stefan asked her to wait a minute, but something inside him hesitated and he asked Amanda to stop. As she turned around, the look in his eyes concerned her.

"Amanda, I'm not sure I want to go."

Trying to make light of his fear, she said, "What are you, chicken? A guy that builds skyscrapers, that rides elevators up 40 floors in a little tube, is scared of walking on a huge mountain?"

Stefan smiled and felt a little more at ease.

"You got this. I got your back."

Stefan reached over, held the side of her face and gave her a kiss. They started making their way up the south side. The ascent was still a 20 degree angle, but in some places, it was as steep as 30 degrees. There were a lot of twists, a lot of paths that went around boulders that stuck out, so it was a hard climb. However, the Boy Scouts actually use this route, so there's nothing for Stefan to worry about, and nothing to concern Amanda. This was a climb she had done thousands of times. Her friends would boast she could scale it blindfolded.

They climbed about halfway up the mountain and they stopped to rest. They were right at treetop level, so it looked like they were sitting in the grass when they sat down and saw the tops of the trees. It was like being on the edge of a lake, or a field. They took out their snacks and water and took a break.

Stefan explained to her that he never fully understood what Boston meant when they said they wanted the wilderness to become their city. A building was going to be an example of Mother Nature to those who appreciate the wilderness. He told her, although he had imagined in his head what the building would look like, he felt totally different now. He wouldn't say confused, but he was compelled to be even more concerned about the appearance and the way the building felt from a distance.

"Amanda, I don't believe you understand how deeply you have moved me, how you've opened my eyes to see the creations God has made." The idiosyncrasies, the unique facets of everything that makes up this world all compelled Stefan to believe.

"And I owe that all to you. I would have never seen that. I would have gone through life with money, fame, and never truly been happy had I not met you."

Amanda's eyes filled with tears as she told Stefan how lonely she had been. She explained that she had lost Bobby in a terrible car wreck, and since that day she had never given herself to another man Stefan was the first. He caused her to feel things that she had not felt in over six years. They embraced and held each other tight. He wiped her tears and kissed her deeply. It seemed Amanda was wrapped up in the possibilities of what was to be and she didn't notice what truly was going on. In the distance the clouds were beginning to form.

Amanda never intended to get emotionally involved. She never intended to pay more attention to the person she was with than her surroundings. Now, Stefan was just the opposite. Stefan was always aware of what was going on around him, the conditions in which he was working.

But, he didn't know enough about climbing or Eagle's Nest, to see the signs of danger. They were an hour up the mountain, sitting three quarters of the way from the top, at the edge of the trees. In the distance, the clouds were starting to mesh together and become a single mass.

After their embrace, Stefan said, "We'd better get going. It's getting late," so they continued to climb upwards.

She said, "It's only about another hundred feet and we'll be at the summit," As they worked their way up, Stefan felt the need to tell her how beautiful she was.

So he would say, "That step is because I think you're the most beautiful woman in the world. That step is because you make my heartbeat. That step makes me want to race ahead just so you're coming towards me. That step…"

Amanda cried out, "Stop it. You're going to give me a big head."

Stefan reached up, grabbed her arm, stopped her in her tracks and kissed her deeply and passionately.

He said, "I will give you the world, not because I own it, but because you deserve it."

Again, she became emotional. Again, she was oblivious to what was going on around them. They stood there and talked. They were almost to the summit, almost to the highest peak of the mountain. The dirt was gone and now they were on pure rock. They only had another 40 yards to go and they would be able to see the whole world. She took him by the hand as they started winding their way up the mountain.

Once they reached the top, the view was no less magnificent than the day before. It was miraculous. They sat down on a boulder that protruded on one side, and looked around. As far as he could see, there were other mountain ridges. The trees looked more like water flowing beneath the mountains than foliage. Amanda sat between Stefan's legs. He held her in his arms and pointed to the setting sun.

When he asked her as he pointed to the left, "Is that Boston?" Amanda didn't reply in the way that he had hoped.

She said, "Oh my God. How did I not see that?"
Stefan felt her tense, and his heartbeat dropped because he knew something was wrong.

She said, "We've got to go. Stefan, we've got to go now."

On the left side of the mountain, the side they could not have seen, clouds had formed and they were as black as the night.

She had been so engulfed in his affection, and the thrill of being with him that she did not notice the danger that was creeping from below.

"Stefan, we've got to go. We've got to go now. We've got to get off this mountain."

Stefan was worried. He didn't understand.

He said, "It's just rain, Baby. It's just rain."

"No, Stefan, you don't understand. We are on a slick surface. When these rocks get wet, Stefan, the surface is like soap. It is very hard to keep your footing. We need to get off this mountain now."

There was a bit of frantic in her voice. Stefan knew she was scared. Here's a person who climbed her whole life, who wasn't afraid of bears, wasn't afraid of wolves, but she was afraid of that black cloud. There was something about that black cloud that scared her to the point her voice changed.

"Okay, let's go. Let's go. We'll go right now. Let's go." They started their descent.

They were six hundred feet from the safety of the forest floor. The hope was that they could get to the area that would provide protection, the dirt at the edge of the base of the mountain. They had 600 feet of rock to maneuver before they reached safety.

149

Stefan could tell that Amanda's pace was faster than when they descended the night before. There was no joking around, no conversations about 'catch me if you can.' Amanda was doing her best to get Stefan and her off the mountain before the rain came. He could see the panic in her body. Occasionally, she would look over her shoulder in the direction of the black clouds. They climbed down to about 150 feet, when Stefan felt the first raindrop hit his right shoulder. He was scared to tell her. He kept climbing and then another one hit the side of his neck.

He simply said her name, "Amanda..."

"I know, Stefan. I know. I feel it too. Hurry... We've got to get off this mountain."

They started moving faster. What Stefan found beautiful moments earlier, he now found horribly frightening. All of his fears of heights came back; the nightmares were now very real. He was on top of a mountain, in a world that was fixing to turn as slick as soap, and no way to hold on.

The trees which once seemed like grass, now seemed like shard pieces of glass beneath them. He was petrified. The rain started coming down. It felt cold against the skin, against the goose-bumps on his arms. Each step now was out of desperation.

Amanda called out, "Stefan, make sure you hold on tight. Make sure that you grip the rocks. Don't just hold them loosely. Make sure you grip them tight, Stefan."

She was no longer talking like a woman in love, but like a woman who was scared. She was sharing her fear, letting him know that things were only going to get worse. They were making their way down. She was only 4 feet in front of him, as the rain came down harder and harder.

Just hours before, water ran sensually down his back as he made love to her in the shower, but now water brought fear and anxiety...now he was petrified. The woman he loved was too far ahead to touch. The one thing that kept him safe was becoming wetter and wetter; the rock beneath him was becoming slippery.

"Hurry Amanda... Hurry… Let's get out of here," Stefan cried out.

"Come on baby. We're almost there. We are almost there," Amanda said.

Stefan looked towards the rock and gripped it as he made his way from left to right in a small gap that dropped off 30 feet to the next set of rocks. Amanda had already passed through.

He felt like they were safe. They were getting closer to being able to take it easy and not worry, in the comfort of the trees, because at the edge of the trees the ground came up to the mountain and there was gravel and dirt that absorbed the water. The gravel and dirt floor at the tree line gave you something to walk on like bathroom tile, similar to the little textured butterflies in the bottom of a bathtub. Even though the bath is slick, the butterflies kept you from falling. Stefan knew they only had 200 feet to go.

He could not see very far ahead. The rain made it impossible to see more than 10 feet in front of him. Since they were descending around the side of the mountain, there were moments when Stefan lost sight of Amanda. Although he was following close…four to six feet apart, he still lost sight of her every once in a while. Each time, he would gasp when he looked up and she was not there.

Amanda screamed Stefan couldn't find her.

He looked down the path and she was not there. Amanda had slipped onto the edge of the path, and was barely hanging on to the rocks.

"Stefan...Stefan… help me!" She was laying on her side with her waist over the edge of a 20 foot drop. She was holding on for dear life. Stefan got to her as quickly as he could. He reached out and she put her hand in his hands but there was nothing to leverage against. Amanda understood her situation. She told Stefan to sit down and lean back.

She kept telling Stefan, "Hold on, don't let go. Don't let me go. Hold on, Baby… Let me get my foot back on the ledge and I'll be okay."

Amanda tried to work her way back to the edge of the walkway, but she kept slipping more and more. Stefan was so scared he started to cry. Now the rain came down even harder, he had trouble seeing her face, though she was only an arms distance away.

Stefan was leaning back, sitting on the trail... He lost his balance, falling sideways... He felt his ribs crack as they struck against a rock's edge. She slipped further down his arm, her nails cutting into his skin.

She screamed out, "Stefan… Stefan please hang onto me, don't let go...please Baby please!"

Everything he had feared his whole life was coming true. He finally met the woman of his dreams but now his nightmare, his fear of heights was taking her away. Her arm glossed slippery with the water. He could hear the panic in her voice.

Stefan kept telling her to hold on, "Baby hold on. I've got you, hold on."

But, the rain made it impossible to pull her up. He could barely see her face.

Then, suddenly, like lightning, his hands were empty and her screams filled his head, his heart and soul.

He cried out her name over and over—but she didn't answer.

"Oh my God... Oh my God—Amanda... Amanda!"

"No... Amanda... No!"

He cried out her name over and over, but all he heard was the water pounding against the rocks.

He didn't know what to do. A man who planned everything in his life could not have planned on an accident so severe. He lay against the rock so scared he was shaking. He was numb; he sat there frozen in agony. He was scared to move forward. His ribs made it hard for him to breathe. There was no sound from below. Slowly, Stefan made his way down the mountain. Like a fighter who had been beaten to the brink of death, or a soldier who had been shot over, and over, he was beyond distraught. He reached the SUV and dialed 911.

They patched him through to the forest ranger, which dispatched a helicopter and search crews. When the ambulance arrived and the paramedics finally found him, he was in a fetal position on her side of the car crying.

They took him to the hospital while the rangers searched into the night.

The helicopter had no visibility. The ground crews had trouble accessing that side of the mountain due to the heaven rain. Stefan was sedated, because he was in a state of shock. The next morning, the only thing he heard was the sound of the heart monitor.

The terrible news of the accident was on the television at the nurses command center, broadcasting the details of his tragedy.

The media reported that, "Environmental engineer, Amanda Wilson was believed to have been killed in a tragic accident at Eagle's Nest while on a hike with her boyfriend, famous architect Stefan Rogers."

The media was making the most of the story. It was on every radio and television station across the country. People were talking about it as a Romeo and Juliet tale…a modern tragedy.

Peter Campbell, an expert climber and guide said it best. "Sometimes it is better to climb alone than with someone that can distract you. The mountain has no mercy and if you make a mistake it can cost you your life. I have been the route they took and though it is safe in good weather, in bad it is very dangerous. In the rain we just had... that would be the worst place in the world to be. Hell, I am surprised we are not looking for two bodies instead of one." Though the media played both sides of the story, hope was truly only a dream.

All the nurses knew the story before they even came into the hospital. There was not a dry eye in the building.

When Stefan woke up from sedation he started calling out for Amanda, he tried to get up... he became combative with the nurse,

He cried out "I have to see Amanda... Where is Amanda?"

Stefan struggled to get out of bed, the nurse tried to calm him down but Stefan only wanted to find Amanda.

"Amanda! Where is Amanda? Why won't you answer me?"

The young nurse assigned to his care tried to calm him down. She had just gotten married a couple weeks ago so to see Stefan in so much pain over love got to her. She was not able to control her own tears.

"She is not here Stefan. Please calm down everything will be okay."

Stefan continued to try and get out of bed. The young nurse was too small to physically stop him. She had to push the help button. Several nurses came into the room to help restrain him. Stefan was confused, distraught and in agony. He continued to ask for Amanda.

"Please let me see her. Please!"

The nurses strapped Stefan down but he still was emotionally distraught and out of control; in fact he was getting worse. His struggle to get up had the doctors worried about further internal damage so they decided that for his own good, they would have to sedate him again. A room that was filled with a desperate man trying to find his love became quiet. The nurse wiped the tears from her eyes and stood there looking at Stefan; she felt his broken heart. She was hoping that her shift would end soon. She had been a nurse for many years but never had she been so moved by a patient; never seen a man so in love, so longing to see a woman.

Who was going to tell him they had not found the body? Though the search parties where still out there, the forestry division announced that at this point given the height of the fall, the amount of time that had passed and the location of the accident it now would be a recovery mission. The media had already announced her certain passing… No one could have survived a fall from that high up. For death to be official a body has to be recovered. Sometimes in life the unknown is known… we just don't want to admit it.

The doctor came in the room and looked at Stefan's chart. The nurse did her best not to show emotions as the doctor asked if there was any more word on the girl.

"There still looking… but they said it is a recovery mission now."

The doctor shook his head, and told the nurse,

"What a shame… That boy had everything…what a God awful tragedy…just awful."

www.ingramcontent.com/pod-product-compliance
Lightning Source LLC
Chambersburg PA
CBHW070928130626
46555CB00001B/331